THE BRIGHTSTONE SAGA

BOOK II

THE FORTUNE-TELLER

Paul B. Thompson

 Enslow Publishers, Inc.
40 Industrial Road
Box 398
Berkeley Heights, NJ 07922
USA
http://www.enslow.com

Library of Congress Cataloging-in-Publication Data
Thompson, Paul B.
  The fortune-teller : book II of the Brightstone saga / Paul B. Thompson.
    p. cm. — (The Brightstone saga ; bk. 2)
  Summary: On the run from the evil wizard Harlano, who is after the precious magical
head, Orry, in Mikal's possession, Mikal and Lyra, with the help of a werewolf, are
determined to stop him.
  ISBN 978-0-7660-3983-4
  [1. Magic—Fiction. 2. Werewolves—Fiction. 3. Fantasy.] I. Title. II. Title: Fortune
teller.
  PZ7.T3719828Fo 2013
  [Fic]—dc23

                                        2012005214

Future editions:
Paperback ISBN 978-1-4644-0265-4
ePUB ISBN 978-1-4645-1169-1
PDF ISBN 978-1-4646-1169-8

Printed in the United States of America

082012 Lake Book Manufacturing, Inc., Melrose Park, IL

10 9 8 7 6 5 4 3 2 1

Cover Illustration: © Duncan Long.

CONTENTS

CHAPTER 1

THREE HEADS

Autumn was a taste in the air. Summer and winter were feelings, hot or cold. But fall was a taste, a hint of smoke from hearth fires, the tang of cider on the tongue, and the flavor of the air as heat gave way to approaching chill.

Leaves on the trees were losing their green in Periskold. The northernmost kingdom in Caddia, Periskold was all forest and hills, rocky rivers and crashing coastlines. People there were lumberjacks and miners. On wooded farms, Periskolders raised apples by the ton and kept bees in uncountable swarms.

Today, the farms and mines were empty. Axes were still and the saws silent. Out of the forest and down from the hills, people came to the Fair. Like morning frost and gilded leaves, the Miracle Fair was a sure sign of autumn.

Lots of traveling shows crisscrossed the land. This corner of Periskold was the domain of Anglebart's Miracle Fair. Led by the Great Anglebart himself, the Fair had tramped the shaded lanes of Periskold for forty years. It boasted a caravan of twenty-nine wagons, carrying the equivalent of an entire village—one hundred sixteen men, women, youths, and children. Anglebart knew the best places to camp. Every clearing, every spring, every rare meadow was mapped out in the old man's head. He returned to the same spots year after year. Local folk recognized these places as the Fair's. The map of southern Periskold was dotted with Fair Meadows, Fair Hollows, and Fair Springs.

Anglebart's company was on its fourth day in Fair Hollow, near the village of Axehold. The take had been good. Loggers and their families came out every day, bought trinkets, lost money at the games, and visited the Fair's attractions. Some had not changed in many years. There was Warvo, the Iron-armed Man, and Cheela, Mistress of Beasts. Few living in Periskold had not heard of Temjin the Fire-Spitter or Siniha, the Smallest Woman in the World.

Less famous were the occupants of a small, square tent pitched at the end of the Row of Wonders. Faded red canvas gave no clues as to what lay within. A curious sign hung over the door flap. On it were a star, a jagged bolt of lightning, and a crown, carefully drawn in muted gold on black. Lightning was a universal symbol of magic. The star and crown were less easy to understand. Maybe that's why in the first few days in Axehold, few found their way to the faded red tent.

6

Curiosity eventually brought people to the tent. At the door flap (which was kept closed), visitors were greeted by a short, slight girl in boy's homespun trousers, a white blouse, and a worn green velvet vest.

"Greetings, seekers of knowledge!" she whispered dramatically. "Do you dare enter the place of the oracle?"

Her manners and gestures were impressive, but her humble looks did not match her words. Most people answered, how much?

"A silver mark for one turn of the glass," said the girl. Some paid and went in. Others shrugged and moved on. Those entering heard the girl mutter as they passed, "No refunds."

Inside the tent was a dim single room. A thin candle burned in a holder hanging from the tent's peak. There was nothing else inside but a boy in a long brown robe and a veiled figure sitting behind a small table. A close look revealed the table to be a cider keg, topped with a bit of plank. The keg still bore a twin ring mark scorched into the wood, the mark of second-rate apple cider. On the plank was an hourglass filled with bright white sand.

"Welcome, seeker," said the boy. He turned the hourglass. "What would you ask of the oracle?"

Of modest height, the boy was too young for a beard. His dark hair was cut close to his head, a southern style not often seen in Periskold.

Axehold folk were not complicated. They asked about two things: love or money. Will I find love? Does he (or she) love me? Will I have money? When, and how much?

Once the questions were asked, the fortune-teller stirred. In the low but steady candle glow, his face was barely visible behind a sheer veil. Anyone with good eyes could see pale skin and dark eyes. The fortune-teller had a round belly. From neck to toe, a dark blue satin gown covered him. His hands were clasped over his stomach. He scarcely moved at all.

In low, gentle tones the oracle spoke. His answers were clear and sounded honest. He did not quibble. He did not use clever, ambiguous words to fool the seeker.

Yes, you will find love, but not with her. No money was coming your way for a long time, so be thrifty. He does not love you and never will. Do you know a boy named Cascar? He loves you well.

His advice did not always sit well. Angry patrons sometimes had to be soothed by the boy attendant. If anyone made trouble, Anglebart's men would throw out the unhappy truth-seeker.

As time passed, word went around that the fat fortune-teller was genuine—his predictions came true. *Always.* Good or bad, he was never wrong. By the end of the Miracle Fair's stay, there was a line of Axeholders waiting to see him. Late at night, when Anglebart came with his lantern to announce the closing of the Fair, there were still people waiting to see the mysterious oracle.

When the last Axeholder was shooed home, the boy and girl sagged to the trampled grass outside the tent.

"We're not charging enough," she said.

The boy yawned. "We charge enough, Lyra. These are working folk, not lords and ladies. Some of them come back half a dozen times." Six silver marks was a lot of money for a lumberjack or sawyer to spend on anything.

"Yeah, but old Anglefish takes a big cut of what we make."

"That's the bargain we made." He yawned again. "I'd better see to our friend. Will you fetch supper?"

"Sure, Mikal. Sure."

Lyra bumped around in their baggage behind the tent a moment, then returned with a tin pot and a big wooden spoon. She set off for the bright campfire that marked the Fair's communal cook-pot. Mikal watched her dragging her feet as she passed the other tents. Anglebart's other performers emerged, bowls in hand, and joined the procession.

Mikal slipped inside the tent. The rotund oracle did not stir. He said nothing. Mikal removed the hourglass and plank, then reached inside the keg. He stood up holding a tiny copper bottle with a strangely pointed top.

"Ready for dinner?" Mikal said, gently removing the fortune-teller's veil.

"That's not food, nor do I eat," he said.

"Yes, yes."

The boy applied the bottle tip to the fortune-teller's lips. A glistening drop of oil came out. He put more oil on the oracle's jaw and was about to apply some to his eyelids when the tent flap flew wide. Wind rushed in, almost strangling the candle.

"Watch out, Lyra!" Mikal said. "You'll blow out the light!" Less sharply he said, "What's for dinner?"

"I do not know," said an unfamiliar voice.

Mikal whirled, shielding the oracle with his body.

"Who's there?"

"A patron, seeking knowledge of the future."

He was no Axeholder. His words were too polished. Against the dark tent, all Mikal could see was a dim figure, draped in a long cloak and wearing a cowl.

"We're done for the day. Come back tomorrow."

"No, now is the time."

There was something about that voice . . . Mikal gnawed his lip. Where was Lyra? Where was Anglebart and his roustabouts?

"Stay where you are," Mikal said, swallowing. "I have only to shout and Fair hands will be here."

"There's no need for shouting." The cowled figure stepped closer. Candlelight washed over him. He pushed the hood back from his head. Mikal felt the ground give way under him.

"Master Harlano!"

"Good of you to remember me," he said, smiling. Mikal remembered that smile. It usually meant pain and torment for someone. In this case, probably him.

His dry lips parted to yell. Harlano held up a hand, fingers spread.

"Do not cry out, please. Upon my word as a wizard, I mean you no harm."

Mikal did not yell. His eyes darted to the door. Where was Lyra? She should be back soon. Lyra could be counted on to call for help, regardless of the danger.

"Your word meant nothing in Oranbold," Mikal said. "You lied to the Guild masters and started a war!"

Harlano folded his hands under his cloak and tried to look benign. "A mistake I would not make again. But I am here for another purpose—"

He stepped forward. Mikal retreated, bumping into the fortune-teller's broad belly.

"I am looking for the Sungam head," Harlano said calmly. "Orichalkon, it calls itself."

"I haven't got it."

Harlano smiled. "Of course you do."

"It burned up when you torched the Guild hall in Oranbold!"

"No. It's here in this tent. Behind you, in fact."

It seemed foolish to carry on denying the truth. Mikal slid sideways, revealing the oracle of the Miracle Fair.

Orichalkon was a human head built of bronze. The wizard Sungam the Smith had made him centuries ago.

Perched on an oversized body stuffed with straw, Orichalkon—Orry, for short—was disguised with a horsehair wig and white face paint. It was the same stuff Cheela used to make herself look younger, and Temjin employed to make himself look cleaner.

Harlano chuckled at the sight. "If the masters of Constant Working down the ages could see this! The finest artifact of our art, painted and stuffed to tell fools' fortunes at a traveling fair!"

A loud voice outside drew Harlano and Mikal's eyes to the door. Lyra swept back the flap. She had a steaming pot in one hand and juggled bottles of cider in the other.

"You'll never guess who I saw—" she began. It took only a heartbeat for Lyra to recognize their visitor.

"Fate and Fury!"

She dropped the bottles and pot. Her hand darted under her vest and reappeared gripping a leather sap. Mikal was amazed. He had no idea Lyra had a weapon.

"Peace, girl," the wizard said soothingly. "I am here to do business, not mischief!"

"You're going, right now," Lyra replied. "Head first or feet first!"

"I can't talk before this urchin," said Harlano to Mikal. "Come out. Let us speak together, man to man."

For a long, painful moment the three of them stood, facing each other and not moving. At last, Mikal broke the stalemate. He went to the door. Harlano followed.

"You're not trusting this—this—" Words failed her. "He tried to kill you! More than once!"

Mikal had not forgotten. He decided it was better to hear the wizard outside, away from Orry and hotheaded Lyra. As they slipped out, Mikal muttered, "Get Anglebart."

Outside, the night gripped the meadow well, roofing the clearing with a ceiling of stars. Mikal and Harlano walked side by side, more than arm's length apart, to a stout maple tree on the near side of the meadow.

"Speak, master, and be quick. Anglebart does not like trouble at his Fair."

"You've grown up since last I saw you," Harlano said. Last time he saw Mikal, he had set a swarm of fire-wints loose to burn the Guild of Constant Working's hall in Oranbold, and Mikal, too.

The boy folded his arms. Wind stirred the browning leaves.

"I am ready to put a goodly amount of treasure in your hands for Orichalkon." When his offer got no response, Harlano decided to be more exact. "A thousand Periskold marks." Still Mikal stared, silent. "In gold."

A thousand gold marks was a fortune. Mikal knew from working at the Fair the exchange in Periskold was one gold mark to forty silver. Forty thousand silver marks . . .

"What do you say?" Harlano asked.

Barely thinking about the consequences, Mikal quickly replied, "No."

"Two thousand, then."

That was a mistake. A boy like Mikal could not expect to see five hundred gold marks in his entire life. A thousand gold pieces was an enormous sum. Doubling it sounded impossibly large.

"I can't do it," Mikal said, moving away from his former master. "Orry is my friend."

He tensed himself to run, to dodge, to get away from Harlano's magical wrath. Instead of a terrible spell, the wizard simply smiled.

"Ah, well! I tried to buy it fairly. Farewell, Mikal the smith's son. I regret troubling you."

With a flourish of his cloak, Harlano departed into the night. He did not go ten steps before melting into the deep shadows under the trees.

Mikal swallowed hard. Was that it?

Lyra touched him from behind. Mikal yelped.

"What are you doing?" he demanded.

"Where's the bad wizard?"

Mikal surveyed the darkness. "Gone. I turned down his money, and he left."

"How much money?" He told her. Lyra smacked her pal with her sap. "Two thousand gold pieces? For that old head?"

Lyra walked past him a few paces, searching the night herself.

"Old liar. I don't believe it," she said. "Harlano give up? He'll be back. He will be back."

CHAPTER 2

FOUR FEET

It was hard for Mikal to put his head down that night and sleep. Lyra didn't help. She went on and on about the dire things in store for them, now that Harlano had found them.

Mikal slept on a bedroll on one side of the tent. Lyra had the other, while Orry sat on his rotund body all night between them. Mikal had grown used to the random clicks and whirrs Orry made in the night, but after Harlano's visit, every sound he heard was alarming. Lyra snored away, uncaring. Mikal wondered how a girl who had grown up in the streets of Oranbold, living hand to mouth, could sleep so carelessly. He decided it must be because she had no burdens on her mind.

Slumber did come, but so quietly Mikal didn't realize he had fallen asleep. He dreamt he got up in the morning to find everyone at the Miracle Fair had been turned into a statue. That was one of Harlano's favorite spells; "petrification" it was called. Mikal wandered from tent to tent, noting with horror each familiar face he found frozen in stone. Siniha, the tiny woman, looked like a votive statue, the kind Periskolders put on the graves of their ancestors. The powerful Warvo had been caught in midstretch as he performed his ritual exercises. Cheela was frozen next to her favorite bear, Brander. A fly crawled across her unmoving hand, flew off, and alighted on her face. It crept over her nose to her eye, and still Cheela did not move—

Mikal awoke, cold and sweating. His heart hammered. He opened one eye in time to see Lyra being dragged out of the tent feet first by two shadowy figures. She was limp as a noodle, not fighting back or cursing.

Before he could do anything, strong hands threw him over on his back. Mikal's eyes were open.

"Here! He's awake!" said the man standing over him. He had an odd accent, not from Periskold.

A second man, bearded, with a blood-red scar on his cheek bent down and pressed a strip of parchment to Mikal's forehead. Immediately, his arms and legs went slack. His tongue lolled helplessly on his mouth.

"That's what the casting is for, idiot!" Scarface hissed. "Get him out of here."

The fellow with the odd accent grabbed Mikal's bare ankles and dragged him to the door.

"Don't shake the casting loose!"

Mikal understood a spell, written on parchment, was stuck to his and Lyra's heads. It kept them still and unable to cry out. If the slip of parchment came off, the spell would end.

Outside there were more men with lit torches—and Harlano. He sized up his captives a moment, and then said to the scar-faced man, "Get the head."

"What about them?"

"I have some questions for them," said the wizard. "But if they move, cut their throats."

Mikal wanted to scream for help, but could not make a sound. Questions? Harlano would not ask kindly, and if he didn't like what he heard, cut throats were likely either way.

The boy tried to squirm and shake, but the spell weighed his limbs down. Out of the corner of one eye, he could see Lyra, eyes shut and limp. Poor girl, she probably hadn't even woke up.

Scarface emerged with Orry. At Harlano's order, he pulled off the wig and scrubbed at the makeup with his sleeve. Under the white paint, bronze gleamed.

"Very good," Harlano said. "Now burn the tent."

The man with the odd accent took a torch from one of his comrades. He was about to apply the flame to the bottom of the faded red fabric when a stone the size of a man's fist whizzed out of the dark and smacked into the back of his skull. Without a word, the man spun around and fell, dropping his torch in the dewy grass.

In an instant, Harlano's band was surrounded by angry, shouting Fair folk. They rose up out of the tall grass, dashing out from behind the tents, swinging axe handles and cooking spits. Harlano's hired men had clubs and knives, and Scarface wore a sword. The intruders formed a rough circle around the wizard. Harlano stood there, between the unmoving boy and girl, cradling Orry in his arms.

"What bother," he said. "Earn your pay, Quintane."

Scarface, or Quintane, snapped back, "As you wish, master!"

Warvo and Anglebart led the Miracle Fair folk in a two-pronged attack. Everyone took part, even little Siniha. Spying Mikal and Lyra, Temjin the Fire-Spitter picked the tiny woman up and hurled her over the heads of Quintane's men. She landed like an acrobat, rolled to her feet, and dashed to the helpless Mikal.

"Are you asleep?" she said, staring into the boy's wide eyes.

Eyes wide, he darted his eyes back and forth furiously.

"I guess not. What's this?" Siniha plucked the casting from Mikal's forehead. Instantly, he could move and speak.

"It's a spell! Get the other one off Lyra!"

Harlano was in the way. He was unarmed—in the usual sense—but stood directly in the path of the boy and the tiny woman.

"Watch his hands," Mikal warned. "He uses them to cast spells!"

"Really?" Siniha undid the sparkling cord around her waist. "We'll see about that."

The cord became a lasso Siniha spun over her head. She circled Harlano. Mikal went the other way. The wizard watched the whirling cord with interest, backing up until his heels bumped into Lyra still lying helpless on the ground. He seemed curious, or amused by his position, not threatened.

"Back!" he warned, "or the guttersnipe will suffer!"

Mikal boiled when he heard that. He stooped and found a rock—a nice, hefty stone with sharp edges. Harlano lowered a hand to point at Lyra. Casting her lasso, Siniha caught the wizard's hand. She yanked the line tight. Harlano winced. Orry fell to the ground. Siniha's cord was braided gold wire and sharp.

Mikal flung his rock. Harlano ducked and pulled away, snatching the tiny woman off her feet. Mikal stood over Orry barehanded, daring the wizard to take him back. Harlano glanced at his wrist. Blood ran down his arm from where the cord had cut his flesh. The sight of his own blood unnerved him. He called to his hirelings for help.

All around them, Quintane's men were giving ground to furious Fair hands. At last, Quintane cried, "Save who can!" and the gang broke for the woods—the ones still able to run, that is.

Harlano ran too, pulling at the cord on his wrist. Once he had the wire free, Harlano made a sweeping gesture with his other hand and vanished in a searing flash of light. A violent whirlwind ripped through the meadow, collapsing the closest tents.

Mikal gently peeled the casting from Lyra's face. Without sitting up she blurted, "You let Harlano escape!"

"I don't care," Mikal replied. "Are you well?"

"Well enough." Lyra bounded up. "Good thing I warned Anglefish about the wizard, huh?" Mikal nodded emphatically.

She turned Orry face up with her foot. "You all right, chatterbox?"

"The night is dark, but I am working well," Orry said.

Anglebart came to them, followed by the leading members of the Fair. He frowned at the bronze head lying in the trampled grass.

"Is this what they were after?" he said. He was a big man, with fair, thinning hair and a broad, drooping mustache. Mikal admitted the truth. Anglebart picked up Orry and looked him in the eye.

"You're the fortune-teller. You should've seen this coming."

"No one can see what one does not look for," Orry said.

The Fairmaster snorted and thrust the head on Mikal. Surveying his people he found plenty of bruises, black eyes, and a few broken bones.

"I can't have this. A Fair must be a safe and friendly place. I can't have thugs and wizards attacking my people."

"It's not our fault," Mikal tried to explain. "The wizard, Harlano, used to be my master—"

Anglebart held up a callused hand. "Save your words, boy."

"What do you mean?" Lyra said.

"You're out," Anglebart said, planting his fists on his hips. "You, the boy, and the oracle must go."

"When?"

"Now! When dawn comes, you must be far gone from here. I won't have any more fighting in my camp."

Mikal clamped a hand over Lyra's mouth. Her cheeks were streaked with tears.

20

"We'll go," he said. "Thank you for saving us."

Anglebart grunted. "Can't have ruffians stealing from my people."

He stalked away. The others followed, nursing hurts and murmuring about Orry and Harlano's noisy escape. Mikal heard one of the teamsters offer money on how long he and Lyra would live after tonight. . . .

Furious, Lyra broke free and ran to the red tent. The shelter belonged to Temjin. The keg and plank table belonged to Warvo. Sundial and costumes were the property of Anglebart. All she and Mikal had in the world were two small bundles of spare clothing, an iron cooking pot, and two wooden spoons.

Mikal carried Orry to the tent. He watched in silence as Lyra angrily stuffed their modest possessions into an old square of blanket.

"It's not right!" she said, still crying. "Why do we have to go? It's not our fault Harlano found us!"

"No, it's not, but you can't blame Anglebart. What he said was true. He can't have a rogue wizard stalking the Fair wherever he goes."

She stopped her mad packing. "What'll we do?"

Mikal had no idea. Orry spoke up.

"Farhaven."

"What?" said Lyra and Mikal together.

"The city of Farhaven, on the northwest coast of Periskold. Population, 64,394. A seaport. Principle sources of wealth: fishing, trade, moneylending. Ruled by—"

"Stop," said Mikal. Orry's recitals could go on a long time. "Why should we go to Farhaven?"

"The city has a powerful Guild of Constant Working. Current chief of the Guild in Farhaven is Excellent Imolla, a magician of great skill and long experience."

"Could this Imolla protect us from Harlano?" Lyra asked.

"Without doubt," Orry said.

She leaped up. "Right! Let's go!"

"Wait!" Mikal rubbed his forehead, thinking. "It's a long way to Farhaven."

He had seen the detailed map Anglebart kept in his tent, drawn on a single sheepskin. Farhaven was completely across Periskold, as far away from Fair Hollow as could be in the same country.

"I'm not sure how to get there."

Lyra said, "You know the way, Orry?"

"I know the direction and landmarks on the way," he said.

There seemed little choice. Mikal said. "To Farhaven?"

"To Farhaven!"

Lyra shouldered one bundle and gave the other, empty one to Mikal. He slipped Orry inside the square of cloth and hoisted him over one shoulder.

Outside, all was still. Quintane's men, knocked senseless in the fight, had stolen away. Only the huge campfire in front of Anglebart's tent still blazed. The rest of the hollow was dark. By starlight, they crept silently away. Mikal would miss many of the Fair folk, especially brave little Siniha and her golden cord.

CHAPTER 3

FIVE LEAGUES

They struck out north. There was a good road that ran west from Fair Hollow; however, it did not seem safe to travel so openly. Neither Lyra nor Mikal had any doubts Harlano would come after Orry again.

The way north was a narrow track, deeply rutted by loggers dragging trees to the Tombow River. Big logs were rolled into the water all along the Tombow and floated to a mill town called Heartwood. Warvo the Iron-Armed man, who had been a lumberjack before joining the Miracle Fair, always called the place "Hardwood," because it was infested with so many hard-hearted, dangerous types.

"We should avoid that place like death," Mikal said, tramping along the dark, wooded trail.

"Why? We could set up Orry as a fortune-teller and make some money for food and lodging," said Lyra.

"Harlano will find us for sure if we did that. We must stay small and keep out of the light." Like rats, he added silently.

They walked and walked until they were too tired to go any farther. Lyra was ready to collapse in the ditch, but Mikal forced her away from the road and up into a tall tree.

"I'm not a squirrel," she said crossly, watching Mikal climb.

"Do you want to sleep by the road, where any passing rogue can rob you or kill you? We'll be safer up here."

The ancient poplar tree had wide, spreading branches, easily thick enough for the children to perch on. Mikal set Orry face out in a convenient niche so he could stand watch while they slept.

"How far have we come from the Fair?" Lyra wondered as she settled against the trunk.

"Two leagues? It's hard to tell in the dark."

Mikal remained awake, on watch. Light rain began falling. His breath made puffs of mist in the air. Lyra, on the leeward side of the tree, was dry and sleeping with her usual heaviness.

Dawn was not far off. Mikal shifted, letting his numb parts come back to life. He was about to speak to Orry when he saw the lights.

Below were four small, bright pinpoints, moving slowly on the logging path they had followed. At first, Mikal took them for lanterns, but the flames were blue, not yellow.

Slowly, they came closer. He glanced at Orry, nestled between three rising branches. Mikal was afraid he would say something and give away their position. Orry had one failing: He could not whisper. Everything he said came out loud and clear.

The sky brightened from black to gray. It had rained enough now to make the leaves drip and raise a damp fog. The floating blue lights gained haloes. On they came. Mikal prodded Lyra with his foot.

"Wake up," he hissed. "Lyra! Wake up!"

She moaned a little, too loudly, and hugged the tree. The lights halted.

By now, they were close enough for Mikal to see no one was carrying the strange lights. They were balls of blue fire, floating in the air about head height. Mikal remembered the captive creatures in the Guild of Constant Working's hall in Oranbold. Fools' Fire, they were called. Were these nature spirits loose in the morning rain?

The damp finally reached Lyra. She wriggled under her rough blanket-cloth cloak and muttered something about the tent leaking.

Mikal pushed her hard with his toe. Her eyes snapped open, an angry complaint at the ready. Mikal pointed at the silent intruders below. Lyra bit her lip.

The lights had been strung out in a line, meandering down the path. Now they clustered together into a single bright ball. They were hovering just over the spot where Mikal and Lyra had left the path.

If it comes toward the tree, we'll have to run for it! Mikal thought. *But where?*

The lights remained in place for an agonizingly long time. As Mikal was about to take a chance and leap to the ground, there was a flash of lightning, chased hard by a thunderclap. The tree shook. Orry toppled to the ground. Lyra slid off her branch, dangled for a moment, then dropped too. Only Mikal held on.

Lyra crouched behind the tree. There was nothing to hide from. The lights were gone. Mikal climbed down. Lyra stood there, arms folded hard, shivering.

"Are you hurt?"

"No," she declared. But she shook with fright.

He found Orry. He had landed on his metallic face. When Mikal picked him up, Orry was chewing on a mouthful of wet leaves.

"Magff, mumf," he said. "Flobf!"

"Patience!" Mikal pulled the leaves out. There were a lot of them. "Good thing you can't taste them," he said.

"Who says I cannot?" Orry's eyes clicked as he shot them left-right-center.

Mikal said, "Can you taste?"

"Certainly! I had a mouth full of poplar leaves, moss, soil, and two earthworms." Mikal apologized.

Lyra called to them from the path. She was standing where the four lights had been. Rain dripped off her nose as she pointed to the muddy track.

Pressed in the gray mud were four pairs of footprints. Small, bare footprints, as if children younger than Mikal and Lyra had stood there. Mikal crouched, showing the strange tracks to Orry.

"What were they?" Mikal asked in a whisper.

"Fey folk," Orry said slowly. The cold and darkness was beginning to wear him down. "Ancient inhabitants of the forest."

"Would they do Harlano's bidding?"

"Cannot say. Few humans ever see them. Harlano may have the power to summon them. They are peerless trackers . . . " He left the statement unfinished.

"Why did they leave?"

Orry's bronze eyelids closed. "Fey folk cannot bear strong light or loud noises," he drawled. The lightning flash and thunderclap had driven them off.

Orry ceased talking. He needed sunlight to regain his powers of speech and thought.

Lyra was already trudging away. Mikal hurried after her. The rain fell harder, graying the dawn and soaking the children to the bone.

They heard the river long before they saw it. The rain subsided to a sprinkle, just enough to keep the leaves dripping. When Mikal and Lyra paused for the first time since leaving the tracks of the Fey folk, they heard the loud rush of the Tombow, straight ahead.

Lyra's lips were blue from the cold and damp. Her hair hung in thin strands around her face. Seeing her like that, Mikal noticed her cheeks were hollowing out and her shoulders were wider than he remembered.

The ground pitched down more and more steeply. They had to cling to trees to keep their footing. Abruptly, the ground ended. Lyra, out in front as usual, gave a yell and sat down hard, clinging desperately to a tangle of roots. Warned by her, Mikal got off the slippery path and wedged himself behind a stout cedar.

They were on a bluff overlooking the river. The drop below Lyra's feet was forty paces at least, straight into rushing water. Across the river, they saw a great tree trunk, trimmed of limbs, hurtle down the slope into the air. It plunged down, smacked the water, and bobbed to the surface again.

Mikal cried, "This path—it's a slide for felled trees!"

"So what? I'm not jumping from here!" Lyra replied. Her eyes were wide just gazing at the fall in front of her.

"No, don't you see? A tree like that may come down the path behind us, any time!"

Lyra let out another yell and scrambled up the slope. Mikal was on the other side of the path and couldn't reach her. Cinching the bundle with Orry inside close to his back, he pushed off from the tree. His short Periskolder boots found no footing, and he fell flat. Sliding headfirst for the edge, Mikal cried, "Lyra! Lyra!"

His face and hands dangled in open air. Something snagged his foot.

He gasped, "Lyra! Help!"

"I'm tryin'," she said with a grunt. "You're heavier than a sack of stones!"

Orry slid down his back until the metal head was pressed hard against his neck. He was slipping. Straight down was nothing but swift water.

"Stop wiggling!"

Mikal shouted, "I'm not!"

He felt her small hands on his belt. Mikal wore wide-legged trews, like the other men in the Miracle Fair, and a thick leather belt to hold them up. Thank Fate! At least Lyra had something sturdy to grab onto.

With much grunting and a lot of Oranbold profanity, Lyra managed to draw Mikal back far enough so he could use his hands to help.

"Why in Fury's name did you throw yourself down there?" she said, gasping.

"I didn't. I was—" He found a tree root and seized it like a starving boy taking a loaf of bread. "I was trying to help you!"

Just then they heard voices—loud male voices farther up the hill. In horror, Mikal realized that they were lumberjacks about to send a tree down the path. He struggled harder, twisting to one side and taking hold of Lyra's wrist. A crashing sound above was followed by the snapping of branches and the swish of leaves.

"Move, now!"

With strength he didn't know he had, Mikal doubled over and threw his arms around Lyra. She gripped a sapling with her other hand. With a rumble, an enormous tree rushed by, leaped into the air, and vanished.

"Let go," Lyra said. Mikal, eyes shut, held on. "Let go, you oaf, I can't breathe!"

He opened his arms. Lyra was pale and coughing. Mikal asked her what was wrong.

"Wrong? Did you feel nothing?"

Mikal reached behind his back. The log had passed by so close and so fast it had ripped his shirt. He wasn't bleeding, but Orry was gone. The tree had torn the bundle right off his back and carried it over the bluff, into the river.

CHAPTER 4

THREE ALLIES

L yra had to hold Mikal back. His first impulse was to leap after Orry. "Are you mad? Jump from here and you'll die!"

She was right. Clinging to a trio of trees off the logging path, Mikal gazed down at the swirling current. There was no sign of Orry or the bundle he'd been wrapped in.

"We've got to find him," Mikal said.

"Find, yes. Jump, no."

They worked their way along the edge of the bluff, flinching every time the loggers sent a new tree into the river. There didn't seem to be any way down. Then they came upon a band of lumberjacks trying to free a jammed tree.

Four Periskolders, stripped to the waist and bearing double-headed axes, argued loudly about how to get the tree loose. The great oak log was caught front and back against tough saplings lining the slope. Two of them wanted to cut the oak log in two; the other pair wanted to cut down the saplings.

"Them's elm slippers!" one logger declared. "No bigger than yer wrist, but tough as brass. How you gonna cut 'em on this steep? You'll break yer axe and tumble down t' the Tombow!"

"Ya think it's any softer to hack the oak?" retorted the lumberjack on the other side of the thick, stuck log. "The money's in the log. Would ya change a gold mark for two silvers?"

Lyra cleared her throat. "You boys stuck, eh?"

They stared at the children.

"What in the name of sweet Fate are ya doing here?" said the oak-cutter.

"Trying to get out," Mikal said. "How do we get down to the river?"

"Jump!" said the nearest logger. They broke into rough laughter.

"That's no way to speak to the young sage of Oranbold," said Lyra. For half a moment, Mikal didn't realize she meant him. "Ask him how to fix your problem." She stood back, holding out her hand as if presenting a lord. "He reads *books*."

Playing along, Mikal tried to look wise. Lyra was using the same tricks she had used to lure customers into the fortune-teller's tent.

"Sage, are ya? Well Sage, how do we get this oak into the river without making kindling o' it and not flying ourselves?"

Mikal said, "Why don't you saw the saplings down? That's safer than swinging axes."

The loggers were thunderstruck.

"He's right, Ganther. I'll fetch a two-hand saw from our camp."

The man who wanted to cut the oak log in two started away. Ganther, the lumberjack in the leather jerkin, said, "Hold up, Polo. We'll all go down." To Mikal and Lyra he said, "Come, ya."

The burly Periskolders hauled the boy and girl uphill effortlessly, pulling themselves along from tree to tree with ease. Before they knew it, Mikal and Lyra were on level ground again. They followed a footpath along the top of the bluff. Soon they reached a series of log ladders. Climbing down one notched log after another, they easily reached the pebbled beach alongside the river.

The rumble of moving water had become a roar. Spray drenched the stony ground, making the way treacherous. City-girl Lyra had never seen such a torrent. Neither had Mikal, who hailed from the flat woodland of Phalia.

The Periskolders had no problem walking. Their boots were soled with short gray spikes. Mikal asked what they were.

"Teeth," Polo said.

"Human teeth?" said Lyra, halting.

"Nay, teeth of the ripper fish, from the ocean-sea. We get 'em in trade from Farhaven."

Logs surged by, driven by the powerful current. Mikal thought that if they could ride on one of those logs, they could reach Farhaven in no time. It was far too dangerous though. Logs smashed into each other, into stones in the riverbed, and careened on. Riders would certainly perish.

A high fence of slim logs surrounded the loggers' camp. Thinking of Quintane and his band, Lyra asked if bandits were a problem in the forest.

"Nay," said Ganther. "The stockade keeps out the Fey folk. Lost two men to Fey shot this fortier." The mysterious inhabitants of the deep woods did not take kindly to their trees being cut down. According to Ganther, they sometimes ambushed lone lumberjacks with tiny, stone-tipped arrows, dipped in poison.

Inside the fence were eight log houses, each with a sharply pointed roof, single door, and no windows. Smoke rose from holes in the roof peaks. Polo and the loggers left Mikal and Lyra with Ganther and went to fetch a saw.

"Who's your chief here?" Mikal asked.

"Kenvist. Go to the big hall and look for the man with the biggest beard. That'll be Kenvist. Fare ya well, young sage." With that, Ganther rejoined his comrades.

In the center of the camp was a large, long hut. The children went inside the smoky building. It was mostly empty, as the lumberjacks were hard at work in the forest. Spotting Kenvist was simple: He had a bronze-red beard down to his waist. Did the Periskolders choose their leaders by beard length, or was beard size a badge of authority? Mikal did not know.

Kenvist was totaling the day's bounty on a counting board. This was a square of white wood as wide as both of Mikal's hands, fingers spread. Crossing lines drawn in charcoal made smaller squares. Kenvist was moving stone chips here and there, reckoning the number and types of trees his men had harvested.

"Ten, thirteen, sixteen oak; seven ash; ten, twelve, fourteen elm—"

Mikal saluted, Phalian-fashion.

"My lord, a word if you please."

"Lord? Who's a lord? I work for a living," Kenvist muttered, struggling with his counters. "Nine, eleven, thirteen cedar . . . "

They waited until he finished. Kenvist looked up from his board.

He was a younger man than his prodigious beard suggested. Like Ganther's band, he was surprised to see a boy and girl in the middle of the forest, unescorted and wearing fancy (to a lumberjack) clothes.

"Who be you?"

Mikal made the introductions this time, avoiding Lyra's young sage tale. As he put it, they were on their way to Farhaven, got lost, and then lost a valuable item in the river.

"What item?" Kenvist asked.

"A head made of metal. Part of a statue."

"Did ya now? And who are you running from? Her father or yours?"

That was the second time Lyra and Mikal were mistaken for runaway lovers. Did they seem old enough to be eloping? It made no sense to Mikal.

"It's not like that, chief," Lyra put in. "We have to deliver that head to Farhaven. We're to be paid well when we do."

"Who's payin'?"

Before Mikal could say anything, Lyra replied, "Imolla."

Kenvist's bushy auburn brows shot skyward.

"Excellent Imolla? The wizard?" Both children nodded solemnly. Kenvist seemed to look at them in an entirely different way. "Ya need help, then. The Tombow scours the riverbed hard. There's no sand in it, just rocks."

"The head is bronze, not hollow. It would sink like a stone," Mikal said.

"Weighty, ya? That will fetch it on Tono's Rake."

He produced a crude map of the river, drawn on a roll of birch bark. Tono's Rake was rocky rapids a short distance downstream. Kenvist offered to guide the children there.

Mikal gripped the logger's hard hand. "Thank you! Thank you!"

Kenvist colored. "No worry, ya? Just be sure to mention to Excellent Imolla who helped ya."

Kenvist led them to the water's edge. The river was so loud they could barely hear each other.

"That's the Rake, ya hear!" Kenvist bellowed over the noise. "Come ya."

They clambered over boulders and across spits of mud. The day was sunny but cool, and the air was so muggy their clothes grew damp and heavy. After a long scramble down the south bank of the river, they came to a broad platform of rock, jutting out over the crashing torrent. Kenvist strode out to the end of the ledge and pointed. Lacking spiked boots, Mikal and Lyra crept along, holding each other's hands tightly.

"There!" Kenvist said. They couldn't hear him, but the gesture was unmistakable.

As far as they could see northward, the river was filled with enormous slabs of stone. Some thrust upward, sharp as battlements. Others were pitted with small pools of mossy green water gathered from the constant spray. Down the center of Tono's Rake was a channel hacked out centuries ago. About four paces wide, it was the only open route through the Rake. Periskolders in ages past had chipped out the channel by hand.

"How will we find Orry in all this?" Lyra shouted in her friend's ear. Mikal had no answer.

He started down to the Rake to find his lost friend. He searched in every mound of leaves and branches washed up on the stones. Lyra joined in, though she quickly tired and found a dry spot to rest. Mikal hunted until he was muddy up to his waist. Tired, cold, and hungry, he joined Lyra on her rock.

Talk was impossible. She dug out some very dry and hard biscuits baked days before at the Miracle Fair. Mikal gnawed his, trying to think.

Young sage indeed! He had no idea how to find poor Orry. Kenvist thought a heavy object falling in the river would be rolled along the river bottom by the current until it reached the Rake. Mikal hated to think what that would do to Orry's fine gears and polished joints. He might be battered to pieces.

What if they never found Orry? Life would go on, but what would Mikal do? His and Lyra's only asset was Sungam's remarkable device. Perhaps Imolla would take them on as apprentices. There was no point trying to go home to his village. Harlano would certainly watch for his return there.

Harlano . . . what would he do when he found out Orry was lost or destroyed? The possibilities that came to Mikal's mind were not pleasant—not pleasant at all.

Maybe he was going at this the wrong way. Stop thinking of Harlano and Orry. Suppose it was something else valuable lost in the river. Treasure, perhaps. Gold. How could Mikal find it?

He kicked his memory hard to remember his lessons in Oranbold two years' past. What kind of Brightworking magic was used to find precious metal? Words on yellowed parchment came back to him: *The odor of metals is distinct and strong. Gold is the sharpest, then silver, copper, and tin. Iron has no aroma, but kills the odors of the others. . . .*

That was no help. Mikal could not sniff out bronze, no matter what the ancient texts said.

"The biscuit is gone." Mikal roused from his thoughts. He had two fingers in his mouth.

"Gnawing yourself won't help," Lyra said.

"How do we find Orry?"

"I knew a fella in Oranbold who found things for people."

"What did he do?"

Lyra drew a knee up to her chin. She had to shout to be heard over the water.

"He used a forked stick, like a slingshot, and it led him to things. He was working magic outside the Guild, and when they found out, he was punished." Mikal asked what happened. "They put a spell on him so that any touch of wood gave him welts and pustules."

Mention of a forked stick stirred other memories. What was it the wizard Hazell wrote? *Of dowsing, the worker must try what wood suits his senses. Many use fruit wood, while others declare water-hungry woods are best.*

"Let's find Kenvist," Mikal declared, jumping up.

"For what?" Lyra said, dejected.

"He knows wood, doesn't he? I'm going to make a divining rod and dowse for Orry!"

The loggers' chief was skeptical. Fruit trees were rare in the deep forest. As for water-loving trees, Kenvist showed them a thicket of young willows on the far side of the Tombow. Mikal borrowed a hatchet and set out. Lyra dragged her feet, but she came.

Crossing the log channel proved easier than expected. A steady stream of big logs was forced into the channel by the current. Heart hammering, Mikal bounded across; each time his foot came down on a different log. In moments, he was on the other side.

"Come on!" he called. Lyra shook her head. "What are you waiting for?"

"The rest of my life!" She sat down on the damp stones and would not budge.

Mikal went on to the stand of willows. There were plenty of them, but very few were forked. He finally cut down a sapling with a very narrow split. Hurrying back, he bounded over the log channel as before.

Lyra saw him grinning. "Fool," she said. "One wrong step, and you're drowned or crushed."

"Drowned? Wouldn't you jump in and save me?"

"No."

She seemed angry, and he didn't know why. Mikal didn't press the matter. He had his willow fork. Now to try dowsing for Orry.

CHAPTER 5

ONE FATHOM

Mikal marched to and fro across Tono's Rake, trying to feel any pull on the willow branch in his hands. He felt nothing. Urged to try, Lyra criss-crossed the stone slabs too, holding the divining rod chest-high. On her fourth trip across the Rake, she halted.

"Nothin'," she said.

Disgusted, Mikal told her to give up.

They had been at it all day. By the time they quit, the sun was setting. Light was failing fast, because they were at the bottom of a steep ravine.

"Where are the lumberjacks?" Lyra asked. The shouts, the scurrying men, and the flow of logs from the bluffs had stopped.

"I guess they've given up for the day. We'd better too," Mikal said. He was starving. They'd better get back to the stockade as soon as possible.

Frogs were serenading as they hurried up the path to the loggers' camp. They had to circle completely around the fence to reach the one gate. When they got there, the log barrier was shut. Twin torches blazed above the closed gate.

Lyra opened her mouth to shout. Mikal clamped a hand over it. "Shh!"

Out of the woods came a sturdy woodsman, double-axe on his shoulder. He looked enough like Ganther to be his brother—brown beard, leather vest, and boots. In the clearing before the gate, he paused and lowered his axe to the ground.

"Halloo!" the lumberjack called. "Man at the gate!"

Instead of an exchange of words, the logger who appeared over the gate leveled a crossbow at the latecomer. Without any challenge, he loosed his bolt, hitting the lumberjack in the chest. Lyra almost screamed. Again, Mikal smothered her cry.

The lumberjack dropped his axe, staggered back, and collapsed. For a long time the bowman sat where he was, watching the fallen figure. Then a pair of pale blue lights emerged from the dark foliage.

"Fey folk," Mikal whispered.

Dim shapes stood over the logger. A third glimmering light rose from the fallen figure and joined the other two. Slowly, the lights faded into the surrounding forest.

"Go that way," Mikal whispered. "Keep out of sight!"

The crossbowman on the gate was still watching. The children crept close enough to see what remained of the shot logger: empty clothes, an axe, and a crossbow bolt, poking through an abandoned leather vest.

Mikal understood. The Fey folk tried to slip one of their people into the camp disguised as a human. The guard wasn't fooled, shot the trickster, and other Fey folk came to collect their comrade.

"We can't go in, or even show ourselves," Lyra said, realizing their predicament. "They'll think—"

"They'll think we're Fey folk in disguise, too."

No supper tonight. Mikal began thinking about finding a likely spot to spend the night when Lyra put her nose in the wind.

"Smell that?" she murmured. Before Mikal could answer, she darted away, deeper into the woods.

"Fate, stop!" he gasped. Moving too suddenly, he caught the eye of the alert sentry. A bolt swished by Mikal's shoulder and hit a tree, *thock!*

He ducked down and kept after Lyra. "Stop! Come back!" he said as loudly as he dared.

Following the sound of her footfalls, Mikal thought the girl was mad, dashing off into the black woods. What was she after?

Then he smelled it, too. Woodsmoke, and food cooking. Delicious, tempting food. His belly growled. No wonder Lyra let out. She never could turn down a meal.

Mikal leaned a hand against a tree and listened. He could still hear Lyra cutting through the forest, farther away. The girl could move when she wanted to. Sighing, he started after her.

He never saw the trap. One moment he was picking his way along, bending branches out of the way and straining to hear Lyra. The next thing he knew, he was flat on his back. His feet were tight together and Mikal couldn't separate them. He struggled, but something strong was wrapped around his feet.

Blue lights quietly emerged from the darkness. Mikal tried to crawl away, but his hands were quickly pinned to the ground. Unable to move, he yelled as loud as he could, "Help! Lyra! Kenvist! Help me!"

A dimly glowing object appeared beside his face, pressed hard into the ground. Mikal was able to see it was a spear tip, cunningly fashioned from flint. The stone touched his face, and he promptly passed out.

When he came to, he was being borne along by unseen captors. His head hung down, and he could see Lyra being carried in front of him by four pale phantoms. He tried to lick his lips and cry out, but his throat was as tight and dry as an old boot.

How long they were carried he could not tell. After a time, he and Lyra were lowered to the ground. Fey folk were all around them, vaguely human-shaped, but small, slender, and glowing with an eerie blue light.

A whispery voice said, "Are you of the tree-takers?"

Swallowing, Mikal rasped, "No."

"And the other?"

Lyra moaned. Mikal said, "She's with me. We're not lumberjacks."

"Yet you walk with them, speak with them."

"We needed their help to find something we lost."

"The metal one."

A thrill ran through Mikal. The speaker must mean Orry! He tried to sit up, but it felt as though a heavy weight was on his chest. Struggling, he managed to say, "Yes! The metal one is my friend."

Two specters came closer, and the great weight disappeared. Mikal sat up. So did Lyra. Her eyes were wide. Her face was streaked with mud and her hair askew. Mikal hoped to Fate she would not make trouble.

"It must go. It must go beyond the forest," the whisperer said urgently.

"I don't understand."

"It poisons us. It stains the air. The others, the Aeni, seek it. They will war on us to have the metal one."

Lyra scooted close to Mikal. "Who are you talking to?" she said.

"The Fey folk," he said. To their captors he said, "His name is Orichalkon. You say he poisons you?"

"Metal is poison. . . . "

Mikal explained to Lyra. "The Fey folk cannot bear to have metal around them. It sickens them."

"So give us Orry and let us go," she replied loudly. "We want to leave!"

"The Aeni hunt you and the metal one."

The Fey folk lived in tribes, as the people of Phalia and Periskold did in ancient times. Apparently, the upriver tribe, the Aeni, were trying to find Mikal, Lyra, and Orry. Mikal did not have to be told who had hired the Aeni to catch them.

"We will take Orry with us," Mikal promised. "Downriver, out of your forest."

The shadowy figures around them stirred. Neither of them heard anything distinct, but feathery whispers and scrapings. They huddled close.

"You will go with the metal one," the voice announced. "The Aeni will not have you."

Lyra and Mikal stood. The ring of glowing shapes fell back from them.

"Thank you," Mikal said.

"Take your metal and go."

A break opened in the wall of phantoms. Lyra seized Mikal's hand and dragged him through the gap. A faint trail led through the pitch-black woods, marked here and there with traces of foxfire. Lyra plunged on, almost pulling Mikal off his feet. Presently, they heard the rush of water. The path took them through a deep, narrow crevice down to the water's edge. Fey folk filled the darkness behind them.

"It is there, in the pool. . . ."

Mikal broke Lyra's grip and ran to the water. Boulders and trees had created a snag in the river. All sorts of floating debris were trapped there. Without hesitation, Mikal jumped feetfirst into the black pool of water.

He sank beneath the surface, though his upraised hands were just above water when he touched bottom. About a fathom deep, he thought. Mikal couldn't see a thing. Fortunately, the powerful current was contained by the snag. He doubled over and groped along the bottom.

The back of his hand bumped something. It shifted away. Eagerly he pushed forward and found the object. Hard, round, heavy—Orry!

With a kick, Mikal broke the surface.

"Take him!" he gasped. Lyra grabbed the head. Mikal climbed out, chest heaving.

Lyra cradled Orry in her lap. The nearness of the metal head drove the Fey folk back. Sensing their dread, Lyra held Orry toward them. The phantoms all but vanished into the trees.

"We got him! Thanks!" Lyra held Orry alongside her face and grimaced at the Fey folk.

"Put him down," Mikal said.

Their captors were gone, except for a few faint glimmers deep among the trees. Mikal thanked them again. To Lyra he said, "Let's be on our way."

"What, now? I'm tired as death! Let's find a dry spot to sleep until daybreak."

"Suppose the Aeni find us before then?"

Sullenly, Lyra agreed. They worked their way down the riverbank to Tono's Rake. The loggers weren't felling anything at this time of night, but random logs lurched downstream, bumping through the channel. Mikal watched several logs go by.

Lyra sagged. "What are you waiting for?"

"The right log."

"For what?"

"To ride on."

She uttered a few choice street-words. Neither Fate nor Fury was getting her to ride a log down the Tombow!

"Are you staying here, then?" Mikal said. Lyra didn't answer. "I am going on. The fastest way to escape Harlano's hired stalkers is by river. At night, the loggers won't be sending giant logs along every moment, so this is the best time to ride."

Out of the gloom, a slow-moving log appeared, quite wide. The stub of a broken branch stuck out from the top, making a perfect handhold.

"Come on, city girl. Show me what you're made of."

Lyra spat in the water. "If you can do it, I can!"

They stood close together, Orry wedged between them. When the big log drifted past, Mikal cried, "One and two and go!" They leaped onto the log, straddling it. Landing stung a bit, but the rough bark meant they would not slide off easily. The log bobbed under their weight, slowed, then began to pick up speed again.

Mikal was behind, Lyra in front. She gripped the broken branch, and Mikal gripped her. As they gained speed, he looked back. Atop the black bluffs were many twinkling blue lights. The Fey folk watched them go.

CHAPTER 6

SIX DINNERS

O nce out of the narrow channel, the log picked up speed. The stream was clear of other logs, so they raced ahead, past the torchlit camp of the lumberjacks and onward into the night. It was easier to talk, too. Canyon and rapids made the river rush and roar. As the Tombow spread out, it quieted, though the current remained strong.

"I'm cold," Lyra said. Their legs were in the river up to their knees.

"Sorry." Mikal rubbed her arms and shoulders. "At least we're getting away."

Lyra made grumpy noises and leaned forward against the broken branch. Cold or not, she was soon asleep.

Mikal examined Orry. He was dormant from lack of sunlight, one eye open and one shut. Mikal brushed silt and algae from his jaw hinge. Then he noticed the damage.

There was a deep dent in Orry's left forehead, probably where the log struck him. Light was poor, so Mikal felt the spot. It was a smooth dent and not a crack.

That was good. Bronze could be brittle. A few smaller dents on Orry's neck were the only other injury. Orry's squared-off base was loose. Mikal had no tools to tighten the screws. Water trickled out of the gaps between Orry's neck and the base.

"Sorry, old friend," he said. His open eye stared back wordlessly.

Somewhere along the way, Mikal fell asleep, too. Next thing he knew, Lyra was kicking him awake.

"What?" he grumbled.

"Open your eyes, blockhead!" He did, and she hissed, "Don't sit up!"

He was slumped forward, pinning Orry to the log. Lyra was still leaning on the branch stump. They had reached a wide, still lake. All around them were floating logs. Lumberjacks were walking from log to log, shouting to each other. Most carried long billhooks, poles with a spear-shaped head and a wicked iron hook behind it.

"Here's oak," cried one close by. Two men hammered spikes into the oak log and then attached long ropes to the spikes. Teams of oxen onshore pulled, dragging the desired log to shore.

"Why are we playing dead?" Mikal whispered.

"Do you know where we are?" He said no, he had no idea. Lyra said, "Neither do I! Be still until we do."

Too late. The inspector spied them. "Ya, spikers!" he shouted. "Someone here!"

Men hopped along the bobbing logs. Lyra sat up, shading her eyes from the morning sun. Mikal hid Orry under his sodden shirt.

"Well! Who are you, lostaways?" said the inspector, a young man with a drooping mustache but no beard.

"Lyra and Mikal," said the girl.

"Strange horse you're riding, ya?"

"We come from . . . upriver," Lyra said. "We escaped the Fey folk."

The loggers looked grave. "You were attacked?"

"By a tribe called the Aeni," Mikal said, trying not to stray too far from the truth.

The loggers helped them ashore. With their spiked boots and billhooks, the Periskolders were able to easily walk across the logjam to land. On the clay strand, the log inspector—his name was Urric—noticed the bulge under Mikal's shirt. Since there was no sense trying to hide Orry, Mikal brought him out. He explained quickly that the metal head belonged to the wizard Imolla. Lyra and he were on their way to Farhaven to deliver it.

The great wizard's name had the same effect on Urric as it did on Kenvist. He promised the children every courtesy in return for good mention to Imolla.

The lake was called Perisk's Bowl. To their surprise, Urric told them they had come more than half the distance from Fair Hollow to Farhaven. They had passed the dangerous town of Heartwood in the dark. Their wet, cold trip downriver all night had served them well.

A small town lined the north shore of the lake. It was called Woodhaven. More than a hundred log houses lined the hillside overlooking the lake. Wooden walls, higher and thicker than the simple stockade at Kenvist's camp, surrounded the town.

Urric took them to a large warehouse at the water's edge to meet his chief, a white-haired old woman. Though her face was as lined as an oak tree trunk, she was more finely dressed than anyone the children had seen since leaving Phalia. She had big plug earrings and a circlet set with bright green stones. Mikal was sure the circlet was gold.

"I am Lamiskellar, chief factor of Woodhaven," she said. Mikal did not know what the title meant, but Lyra acted impressed.

She bowed. "We are honored, lady." Mikal stared until she elbowed him in the ribs. He bowed, too.

Lamiskellar asked them where they came from and how they had come to Woodhaven. Lyra did most of the talking. Mikal listened in amazement at the wild tale his companion spun. He and she were apprentices of the Guild of Constant Working, sent by King Fenry II of Phalia to deliver the Oracle of Oranbold (Orry) to Excellent Imolla. Lyra went on at great length about the perils they had faced, finishing with them being hunted through the forest by bloodthirsty Fey folk. They managed to leap aboard a log heading downstream, which brought them to Woodhaven.

Lyra finished her tall tale. Lamiskellar sat silently, so long Mikal felt embarrassed. Why hadn't Lyra simply told the truth?

"Interesting," the old woman said. She snapped her fingers. Two soldiers in mail shirts and flat-topped helmets appeared.

"Escort the children to my hall. There they will remain to await my pleasure."

It sounded to Mikal like they had just been arrested. As the guards took them by the arms, Lyra said, "What are you doing? Let us go!"

Lamiskellar said, "You shall remain in my hall until I can sort out the truth."

"What truth?" Mikal asked.

"There is in Woodhaven a wizard of some repute who came to me a few days past with a tale of theft and flight. He says this metal head was stolen from him. He says there is a reward for the recovery of the head and the arrest of the thieves."

"Harlano!" Mikal and Lyra muttered as one.

Lamiskellar raised an eyebrow. "So you know him? I call that testimony in his favor."

"Harlano is a liar and a rogue!" Lyra burst out. "The Guild of Constant Working has condemned him. Is there no one from the Guild in Woodhaven you can ask about this?"

Turned out there was not. There were only two Guild wizards in Woodhaven. One was dead—struck by lightning out of a clear sky—a fortier back. The other wizard, an apprentice, had gone upriver ten days ago to help the loggers fend off the Fey folk. No one had seen her since.

The children were escorted from the warehouse. Outside was a large lumberyard, where men with saws and axes labored to turn logs into planks and posts. The air was sharp with the smell of rosin. Drifts of sawdust higher than Mikal's head marked the way out to the street.

Woodhaven was busy. Carts trundled back and forth, laden with wood in various stages of preparation. Everyone seemed to have a tool in his hand, often the famous Periskold double axe. Carrying Orry in both hands, Mikal asked the guard what all the hubbub was for.

"Filling orders for timber," said the soldier.

"Who buys all this?" Lyra wondered.

"Florian."

Florian was an island far to the south. From there, its merchant ships and mighty navy reached all parts of Caddia. To build those ships, the Florian Empire needed lumber, a lot of it. Mikal saw now where they were getting it.

"I speak Florian you know," Lyra said. She said a few words in singsong fashion. Mikal didn't know if she was really speaking the language, or just reciting gibberish.

"Know what I said? 'Your mother is a toad.'"

The guard at her side stopped. "What did you say?"

"I said in Florian, 'your mother is a toad.' It must be true, looking at you," Lyra replied coolly.

"You guttersnipe. I'll wring your neck, ya?"

"Ya this!"

Lyra drew back her foot and kicked the guard smartly. She didn't aim for his shin, the natural place to kick a taller person. She kicked him in the knee. He let out a howl and fell to the ground, cursing.

The second guard drew a stubby sword. Lyra grabbed Mikal by the elbow and said, "Come on, country boy! Time to run!"

Run they did, though Mikal had no idea where they were going. Lyra led him back the way they came, with one guard shouting at them and the other trying to get to his feet. People around them stared but did not interfere. Lyra wove in and around slow-moving carts. Sometimes she walked in step with the thick-legged ponies pulling them, and then darted away. They were almost back to Lamiskellar's warehouse when Lyra diverted down a narrow alley. Near the end she tried a shut door. It was bolted.

Grasping the handle, she muttered three short words Mikal did not understand. When she pushed again, the latch gave. She pulled Mikal inside just as the red-faced guard passed the alley looking for them.

In the dark, Mikal gasped, "What are you doing?"

"Staying out of jail."

"But—"

"You heard the factor. Harlano already has her ear. What chance do you think we have? Even if we didn't end up in some dungeon, do you think Harlano will let us get away? We'd end up floating downriver with the logs."

She was right, so Mikal didn't argue. Instead, he whispered, "Where are we?"

"The Guild's hall in Woodhaven."

Mikal almost dropped Orry. "What! How do you know that?"

He could feel her breath on his face as she drew close. "Didn't you see the symbol carved over the door from the street? The stars? This must be the Guild's hall in Woodhaven."

They crept forward, keeping close to the wall. Passing through an open door they saw streaks of light coming in through closed shutters. Lyra stumbled into a table.

"How did you open the door?" Mikal asked suddenly.

"You don't pay attention at all, do you?" Lyra took Orry and set him on the table. "Back in Oranbold, while you were learning to read moldy old books, I was learning useful things, like how to open the Guild of Constant Working's magical locks." Even in the darkness, Mikal could tell she was grinning. "They use the same spell to lock kitchens and pantries. I learned the counter-spell."

His hand touched something by the wall, cold and metallic. A candlestand. He had no fire to light them.

Lyra went to the window. Gently she pried the slats apart. More light leaked in, and the room leaped into clarity. Clearest of all was the frozen figure of a young woman cowering by the far wall.

Mikal and Lyra slowly approached. The woman wore a Guild amulet around her neck. She was turned half-away, an arm thrown up to ward off something. It was plain to Mikal who this was: the Guild wizard apprentice who had supposedly gone downriver to help the lumberjacks against the Fey folk. She had never left Woodhaven.

"Harlano's touch, all right," Lyra said. She did something Mikal would not. Reaching out, she pressed her thumb into the frightened figure's face. "Hard as stone."

They left the poor young woman and explored the empty house. In the larder they found a table set for six. That was odd. There were just two wizards in Woodhaven, Lamiskellar had said. Who were the other four place settings for?

Lyra found food—stale bread, salted fish, some cabbage. Under a stoneware bowl was half a cheese, fuzzy with mold. Lyra found a blunt knife and began cutting off the gray rind.

The cistern was full of water. Jugs lined up like soldiers along the wall. Most were empty, but the last two yielded good cider.

"At least we won't starve today," Lyra said, helping herself. They sat on the floor devouring cheese, bread, and cider. There was no time to rinse the fish, or build a fire to cook the cabbage.

"What now?" Lyra asked, chewing loudly.

"On to Farhaven."

"Harlano's out there, you know."

Mikal sighed. "I know."

"Owowowow," said a voice from the front room. They had left Orry on the table. Bathed in slender beams of sunlight, he had revived.

Mikal ran quickly to his metallic friend. "Orry! Are you well?"

"Owow," the head complained. "I am d-dented!" Mikal related Orry's fall into the river. "Ow," he said again, more slowly. "I am d-dented."

"You said that." Lyra looked him in the face. "Say something new."

"S-Something new."

He had not lost his sense of humor, but a definite stutter had taken hold. Mikal told Orry where they were and what had happened.

"Harlano is here, looking for us. What can we do?"

"We m-must get to F-Farhaven at once and th-th-throw ourselves on the mercy of Excellent Imolla." That was clear, but how? "Use th-the river."

Travel by water was faster than tramping to Farhaven on foot, but was speed the only reason to follow the water route?

"N-No. Har-Harlano's power is diminished by water," Orry said.

All wizards, he said, chose a path once they reached master status. Harlano had chosen the path of Fire, as it suited his personality. One drawback of a wizard of the Fire path was that certain things were resistant to his power—water, for example.

Lyra let out a whoop. "Fury, that's great! I'll swim all the way to Farhaven if it keeps horrible Harlano from making a statue out of me!"

Mikal studied the sunbeams slanting through the shutters.

"Tonight," he said. "We'll go tonight."

CHAPTER 7

FOUR BROTHERS

L ong before dusk, the sun disappeared. Black clouds billowed across the lake, frowning and flashing as they piled up over Woodhaven. Mikal thanked Fate for them. Darkness and rain would be extra cover for their escape.

They helped themselves to whatever they found in the Guild house. It wasn't stealing, Mikal decided. It was important to keep Orry out of Harlano's hands, and they couldn't make it to Excellent Imolla without food and supplies.

Lyra proved to be an adept scrounger. After cleaning out the pantry, she filled a cloth bag with candle stubs, a kitchen knife, a ball of twine, and even a wooden mallet. The bag was full, but Lyra kept looking.

"What are you after?" asked Mikal.

"There's always some, somewhere," she said under her breath. "Where would a pair of women wizards hide theirs?"

She went around the front room, tapping the wainscoting with the knife handle. Mikal followed, puzzled. Lightning flashed through the shutter slits.

"Where, where . . . ?"

Orry sat on the table, his eyes on Lyra. He was not his chatty self. His adventure in the Tombow River had left him quieter than usual, probably because of his stutter.

Lyra stalked toward Orry, knife in hand.

"S-Say," said the head. "What m-mean you to d-do with that?"

Grinning, Lyra reached the table—then ducked under it. Mikal heard a scrape of metal on wood and the girl's triumphant cry, "Yes! It's here!"

He crouched low to see. Pinned to the underside of the table was a small leather bag. Lyra pried out the nails and let the bag drop into her hand.

With Orry and Mikal looking on, she loosened the drawstring and poured the contents on the table. Gold and silver coins tinkled into a small heap.

"S-Splendid!"

Mikal counted the money. Six gold marks, seven silver, and two bronze cartwheels. Not a king's ransom, but a tidy sum for their journey.

"How did you know there was money here?" Mikal asked.

"Always is, unless the house is poor as dirt." Another silent splash of lightning threw shadows on her smiling face.

They divided the coins, Mikal keeping the purse. Thunder made the house tremble. It was time to go. Before leaving, Mikal draped a blanket over the petrified apprentice.

Stealing out the alley door, they made for the lakefront. They hadn't gone ten steps when the rain came down like a wall, soaking them instantly. The few townsfolk still outside sprinted for cover. Mikal and Lyra slogged on.

Skirting Lamiskellar's warehouse, they found the long wharf by the lakeshore. Boats and barges were tied along the boardwalk. Some were plainly empty. Others showed smoky lamplight glowing within their deck cabins.

"Which one?" Lyra said above the drumming rain.

"Any one."

Mikal spotted a keelboat with a carved bear head post. For no other reason than he thought it looked good, he went to the end of the gangplank and called out, "Hail, boatmen! Anyone on board?"

No one replied, so they went to the next vessel, a barge. Men were idling under a wide awning over the center of the barge. The scent of seared meat penetrated the rain. Mikal hailed them.

"What want ya?"

"We're looking for passage!"

"Which way?"

Mikal cupped a hand to his mouth. "Downstream, to Farhaven."

A man got up and came toward them. By the lantern hanging by the gangplank, Mikal saw the glint of metal on the man's chest. Did boatmen wear armor?

The lantern brightened his features. It was Quintane, Harlano's hired thug!

Lyra bolted past Mikal in a flash. Quintane's scarred face paled. He shouted to his men. Boots scraped as they got to their feet.

Mikal kicked the gangplank, and it splashed into the water. Quintane lunged at him, but Mikal was out of his reach.

"Get him!" he roared.

Mikal had little choice but to follow Lyra. Why did she run down the wharf? It might be a dead end. Burdened with Orry and supplies, he lumbered after his companion. It was pouring now, and every footfall sent fountains of water skyward. He glanced back once. Quintane's men were trying to lay a plank from the barge to the dock. It was too short and toppled into the lake.

Cursing, Quintane gathered himself and leaped. He hit the boardwalk. His feet kicked in the water. With a mighty heave he hauled himself onto the wharf and drew his sword.

"Stand still, you rats!" he cried.

Lyra was already out of sight. Mikal had no idea where she went. The girl had a genius for disappearing.

He kept running, past moored boats of every type. On the stern of an oared galley, a white-bearded man stood drinking from a two-handled mug. He saw Mikal splatter past, and then spotted Quintane in pursuit. More of the bandit's men were struggling ashore.

"Trouble, ya?" White-beard said.

"Yes!"

The old man bent down and tossed something from his craft onto the docks. When Quintane arrived, he promptly skidded and fell flat on his back. Mikal never saw what the old man threw, but he waved and shouted, "Thanks!"

And then he was at the end of the wharf. A big barge was casting off, torches blazing at both ends. Mikal slid to a halt a half step from the edge of the dock. Behind him, Quintane's men were coming. When they saw he was trapped, they slowed to a walk. Several laughed unpleasantly.

"Mikal! Mikal, what are you standing there for?"

Lyra was on the barge. She waved.

"Come on! What, are you afraid to get wet?"

It was a silly taunt. He was already soaked to the skin. Mikal hesitated because he wasn't sure he could swim holding Orry. Then he looked back again and saw one of Quintane's men was cocking a crossbow. With that, he leaped feet first into the lake.

. . . and sank like a stone. It was black as scribe's ink down there. Faint flickers of lightning only made the

64

gloom seem deeper. Mikal kicked and swam with his free hand. He wasn't about to lose Orry again in deep water. His head broke the surface. Mikal gasped once, then sank again. He had provisions, tools, money, and a bronze head on him. He was not going to make it back to the surface.

He heard a second splash. Had one of Quintane's men come in after him? Mikal kicked and kicked. He didn't rise, but he didn't sink either. A murky figure swam toward him. He tensed to fight. Lightning flared, and he saw it was Lyra with a length of rope in her teeth. She wrapped it around him under his arms, tied a knot, and yanked on the line. A sudden surge pulled them upward. They broke the surface. Mikal drew a deep breath. Through the rain he saw the barge was towing them. Men on sweeps and poles were propelling the craft away from shore.

Something went *tisk* into the water beside them. Arrows! Quintane's men were shooting at them.

"Haul us in!" Lyra shouted. "Hurry!"

Crewmen took hold of the rope and dragged them swiftly in. Mikal was yanked from the water and left wheezing on deck. Two barge men flanked Lyra and Mikal with bows of their own. They traded bolts with the men on the wharf until the barge drew out of range.

Mikal and Lyra huddled together by the barge's rail, soaked and exhausted. Heavy footsteps announced the arrival of their host.

"Are you right, girl?" he said. Lyra croaked yes. "How is the boy?"

"Swallowed half the lake," Mikal said.

"Be sure to put your half back," said the barge captain. "The lake needs the water."

He helped the children stand. "Makvar, master of the *Four Brothers*."

"Fate bless you for saving us."

Makvar shrugged. "For what you're paying, I'd've landed and fought those brigands hand to hand."

He went forward, leaving Lyra and Mikal alone. Mikal asked, "Paid? Who paid?"

"We did. A hundred gold marks." Lyra whispered.

Mikal choked all over again. "A hundred what? We don't have—"

She clamped a hand over his mouth. "We don't, but Imolla does! Don't you think she'll pay to keep Orry out of Harlano's dirty hands?"

Lyra gave Makvar her gold as a down payment, promising Mikal's half, too. Eyeing his extravagant friend, Mikal found the master of the *Four Brothers* amidships and gave up his gold. Strange, he had money in his pocket less than a day.

Makvar called for blankets. The children wrapped up and huddled by the firepot crackling on deck. Without asking, a crewman put trenchers of hot food in front of Lyra and Mikal.

"Thank you," Mikal said. Lyra dug into hers without a word.

The barge rowed well out into the center of the lake. Rain poured down. Lightning lanced into the water here and there. Thunder struck like clubs on a barrel head.

Makvar came up from belowdecks. He had a tube of clay in his teeth, curiously curved. As the children watched, he packed the bulbous end of the tube with some kind of dried leaves. Taking a burning twig from the firepot, he lit the plug of leaves and drew the smoke into his mouth through the tube. Mikal and Lyra had never seen the like.

"Sweetcress, it's called," the captain said. "It's a seaweed from the seas of the south." It smelled pleasant, but Mikal couldn't understand why anyone would willingly fill his chest with smoke. He'd inhaled far too much smoke from his father's forge to ever want to do such a thing willingly.

"You were lucky, girl. Our cargo was stowed, and we were planning to leave at first light." Makvar drew on his tube. The smoldering leaves glowed and crackled. "If you'd come much earlier we couldn't have helped you until our cargo was aboard." Mikal thanked Fate for that.

"Who's after you?"

"A man named Quintane, leader of a band of rogues," Lyra said.

"I know that name! A mercenary and bandit. Why is such a wicked fellow after two youngsters?"

Mikal let Lyra weave the tale. By the time she finished explaining about Orry, Harlano, and Imolla, Makvar's bushy eyebrows were stuck to the top of his forehead.

"You run in exalted circles," said the captain.

"The chase isn't over yet," Mikal warned. "Until we are under Excellent Imolla's protection, Harlano will hunt us."

Makvar didn't seem worried. He had eleven stout men in his crew, rough and ready fellows used to brawling and hard work. Quintane's band held no terror for them.

"Quintane is only the eyes and hands. Harlano is our own personal Fury," Lyra said.

Mikal shuddered beneath his blanket. She was right. Harlano was their Fury, the evil luck hanging on their heels. If they couldn't stay ahead of him, he would engulf them all.

CHAPTER 8

ONE RAM

B efore dawn, they spotted their pursuers. The crewman steering the barge saw a dark shape in the mist behind them. It did not trouble him at first, as there were many craft on the lake, but the shape became a boat, and the boat became a galliot, rowing hard up their wake.

Quietly, the alarm was passed. Makvar shook Mikal and Lyra awake.

"Your Fury," he said.

Orry suddenly came to life. Eyes wide he said, "Har-Har-Har—!"

"We know," Mikal replied gently. "We'll protect you."

After the night's rain, a heavy mist clung to the lake, warm and wet. At Makvar's command, his men donned leather breastplates and bulky leather helmets. They broke out their sweeps and began rowing. The galliot, a war boat propelled by twenty oars, could steer rings around a barge like the *Four Brothers*. Its hull was painted bright red. A bronze-tipped ram slashed the water as the galliot churned along.

"Will they ram us?" Mikal wondered.

"If they can catch us, they'll try," Makvar said. He buckled on a heavy sword with a long, curved blade. "Fear not, ya? *Four Brothers* is not a daisy to be plucked!"

The galliot slowly closed on them. Mikal saw men crowded on the foredeck, which was walled like a fortress tower. Probably Quintane and his men.

The barge men not rowing piled bows and arrows on deck. Then they brought up from below some heavy timbers, cut and jointed. Under Makvar's practiced eye, they began assembling the timbers into a machine.

Lyra clung to Mikal's elbow. "What's that?" He didn't know, and said so.

The thing grew into a monstrous device as tall as a man, with two arms sticking out the side and bundles of sinew rope in the center. The barge men were tightening the skeins around the arms when a lookout shouted, "Galliot closing on the port quarter!"

After dogging them until the sun rose, the war boat suddenly leaped ahead, white bow wave curling back from the deadly ram.

"Two points to port," Makvar snapped. He was turning toward the enemy? Why?

"Scorpion ready!" called a crewman by the machine. "Load her, ya?"

With a windlass they hauled back a thick bowstring. The device was like an oversized crossbow. An arrow as long as Makvar's arm was fitted behind the bowstring.

"Steady . . . hold your course, steersman! Two points more to port!"

The lumbering barge turned more sharply. Now the two vessels were coming straight at each other on parallel courses, no more than barge-width apart. The scorpion, mounted in the center of the barge, had a clear field to shoot over the rowers' heads.

Arrows and bolts flickered from the galliot. Some hit the water, some passed over, and the rest stuck quivering in the *Four Brothers'* deck.

Makvar handed bows to the children.

"Can you use these?"

Mikal shook his head, but Lyra said, "Give us a crossbow!"

Makvar handed Mikal one and showed him how to cock it with a goat's-foot lever. Lyra elbowed him aside and took the bow for herself.

The galliot lunged at them. The ram smashed into the barge at a shallow angle and skidded along, chiseling jagged splinters off the thick hull. As the two craft rushed by each other, the rowers hastily drew in their oars so they wouldn't be broken off. Arrows flew back and forth.

Lyra tried to level the crossbow. It was too heavy for her, so she ordered Mikal to kneel. Laying the bow on his shoulder, she aimed at the men on the galliot's foredeck. The bow went *wham* and the bolt flashed away. Lyra cursed. She missed.

Someone on the galliot did not. An arrow hit Makvar. He staggered backward and sat down, staring at the feathered shaft sprouting from his chest. His leather armor saved him, but he was bleeding badly. A crewman frantically bound his wound.

The two craft parted. Oars flailing, the galliot practically spun on its own length. The barge plowed on.

A bold voice rang out. "Raise mainsail! Scorpion, target the enemy rowers!"

The bargemen jumped to obey. Mikal looked around to see who had given the orders. Makvar was down, unconscious.

A light mast was stepped in a bracket on deck and speedily raised. The sun had dissolved the morning fog, and a fresh wind was blowing from the east.

The scorpion cut loose with a loud thump. Its huge arrow arced over, hitting between the first two oarsmen on the port side of the galliot. The thick arrow shaft jammed both oars.

"Again! Loose at will! Target the rowers!"

Who was giving the orders? Mikal didn't have time to find out. He and Lyra struggled with the crossbow, getting it cocked and loaded. Kneeling on deck, he let Lyra brace the weapon against his shoulder. This time she said an oath before she loosed her bolt.

There was Harlano on the quarterdeck with two others, probably the steersman and the galliot's captain.

"Hold still," she said. "I'll get him!"

She squinted over the sight so long Mikal thought she forgot to squeeze the trigger bar. Finally, Lyra loosed the bolt just as a swell rocked the *Four Brothers*. The missile flew low—too low—and hit the galliot's rail. It skipped upward and hit the steersman in the leg. He toppled, dragging on the boat's tiller as he fell. The galliot turned sharply away.

"Good shot!" boomed the commanding voice. "Keep it up!"

The wounded man was dragged away. Another took his place, and the galliot came churning after the barge, following right in *Four Brothers'* wake. Wind was pressing the sail, pushing the barge's nose deep into the water. Despite a constant shower of arrows, the galliot rushed on, ramming its beak into the rear of the barge. There it stuck.

The shock knocked everyone down. Lyra bounced up, struggling with the crossbow. Mikal rolled this way and that, trying to find his feet. The bargemen abandoned their oars and filled their hands with swords and bucklers.

For a moment, there was a lull as each gathered himself for battle. Mikal saw the scorpion crew had given up the catapult for hand-to-hand weapons. He grabbed Lyra by the hand and made for the untended weapon.

"What are you doing?" she protested.

"We can work it," he said. "I'm no use with a sword!"

Voices roared as Quintane's men rushed across the galliot's beak. Makvar's men waited, shields locked together, along the barge's stern. At the scorpion, Mikal quickly sized up the mechanism: Hooks drew the bowstring back on a tray, held in place by a ratchet. He hooked the string and began cranking the winch. Lyra laid a long spear in the tray.

The bowstring locked in place. "Ready?" Lyra shouted. Mikal shook his head.

He peered down the shaft of the spear. It was pointed right at the end of the galliot's ram. The brigands were coming. All he had to do was yank a cord, releasing the catch, and the spear would fly.

His fingers twitched. He couldn't do it. The first man across from the galliot would certainly die, maybe the second man too. . . .

Lyra shoved him out of the way and pulled the cord. With a mighty *wham* the scorpion hurled its missile. It flew between the boarders and stuck in the galliot's forecastle, quivering. Three of Quintane's men fell in the water when they threw themselves out its way.

"Load!" Lyra yelled.

"Scorpion crew! Aim for the enemy's water line!" barked the booming commander. They instantly obeyed. The bronze-headed spear tore right through the hull planks. It dawned on Mikal that the galliot was built for light draft and speed, so it couldn't be as sturdy as the thick-skinned *Four Brothers*.

"Again!" he said.

They put two more missiles into the enemy boat. It began to list as water poured in. Quintane's men, fighting on the rear of the barge, heard the galliot crew's warning cries. They backed onto the beak again, fighting the bargemen all the way. Lyra and Mikal cheered their retreat.

Through the chaos a solitary figure approached. It was Harlano, clad in a simple gray robe. Arrows flew at him. He deflected them with casual waves of his hand. Lyra threw herself against the scorpion's frame trying to turn it toward the oncoming wizard.

He raised his clasped hands over his head. Mikal knew what was coming. He put an arm around Lyra's waist and leaped away from the catapult. As he did a ball of fire hit the machine, instantly wrapping it in smoke and flames.

The galliot's list became severe enough that it twisted the ram loose from the *Four Brothers*. The bow was awash. Rowers fled their oars and moved aft. Quintane's men sloshed through rising water to join them. The barge crew jeered. They stopped loosing arrows at the sinking boat and laughingly returned to their oars.

Amidship, Harlano stood alone. Quintane's men parted and went around him on either side, giving the wizard a wide berth. When the water lapped at his feet, Harlano vanished. He simply faded from sight in clear view of everyone, without fanfare or violence.

"I wish I could do that," Lyra said.

The scorpion was a pile of cinders. Around the ruined weapon, the deck and rigging were singed but unharmed. Under sail and sweeps, *Four Brothers* pulled away. Lyra and Mikal watched as the galliot rolled over and sank, leaving the crew and Quintane's men swimming for the distant shore.

A bargeman led them to Makvar, propped up against the bulwark. His chest was heavily bandaged and stained with blood.

"You have dangerous folk after you," he rasped.

"I am sorry for the trouble we have caused you," Mikal said.

Makvar coughed. "I am paid for trouble. How many did we lose?"

Not one of the barge crew was killed, though more than half were hurt one way or another. The scorpion was destroyed. Makvar wondered why Harlano didn't torch the whole barge.

"He wants Orry," Lyra said. "If he burned up the boat, he wouldn't get him."

"Orry said his power was weakened by water. With the galliot sinking under him, he was thinking more about safety than success," Mikal added.

Mentioning Orry made Mikal cast about for him. The impact of the ramming sent the bronze head rolling into a scupper. When Mikal found him, Orry hailed him in a loud, commanding voice.

"You! You were giving orders?"

Orry resumed his usual mild tone. "Ah, yes. I d-did. Don't know wh-why."

He didn't stutter while giving orders, either. Mikal picked up his friend and took him to Makvar.

"Orry saved the *Brothers*," Mikal said. "When you fell, he took command."

"Really?" The wounded captain hefted the head in one hand. "What boats have you commanded, Brassdome?"

"N-none, good c-captain. I d-don't know what c-came over me. Somehow I knew wh-what to do, and said so. L-loudly." Makvar laughed.

Four Brothers continued down the lake a day and a night. At the far end of the lake, the Tombow River was closed by a boom of chain and logs. A stone fortress overlooked the boom. The lord of the fortress, Count Rynelo, made everyone pay a toll to enter or leave the lake. This made him one of the richest men in Periskold.

Four Brothers joined a swarm of vessels waiting to pass through the boom. It was almost dusk, with a growing chill in the air. Longboats nosed among the waiting traders. In each longboat was an officer of Count Rynelo's army dressed in green, white, and gold. His job was to assess and collect payment. Makvar, back on his feet, had his purse ready to pay. When the boat came alongside, the officer did not ask what *Four Brothers* was carrying. Instead, he thrust a sheet of parchment at the captain and ordered the rowers to move on.

"What is it?" Mikal asked when Rynelo's officer was gone.

"I am good with numbers, but my letters are weak," Makvar said. "You're Guild apprentices; what's it say?"

Periskold was another dialect of Caddian, but the letters were oddly shaped. It took some time for Mikal and Lyra to puzzle it out.

"'Know this, by order of His Lordship, Count Rynelo the Second, master of the Tombow: it has come to our attention—'"

"'Our?'" Lyra said. "Is he more than one person?"

"Hush," Mikal replied. "That's the way the high and mighty talk about themselves." Lyra sniffed.

"'It has come to our attention that an item of great value, stolen from Oranbold in Phalia, is within our realm—'"

"Orry!"

Makvar lit his smoking pipe. "Go on, boy."

The rest of the document said the Count's soldiers would search every vessel on the lake for the stolen artifact, called "a head of metal, as from a statue, that speaks as people do." A reward of one hundred gold marks was offered for the head.

The children looked to the master of the *Four Brothers*. He puffed silently.

"You'd best go ashore after dark," he said. "Less chance of being caught, ya?"

"What about your pay?" Mikal asked.

Makvar turned Count Rynelo's parchment over. "I made a bargain with you, and Makvar keeps his word. Write to Excellent Imolla. Tell her of our deal. When I get to Farhaven, I'll present the bill to her. If she is the wizard people speak of, she will honor it."

Lyra grinned. She fetched a charcoal stick from the wreckage of the scorpion and told Mikal to bend over so she could write against his back.

"Why you? I write, too."

"Yeah, but my pen is better than yours."

She scribbled and scribbled. Makvar peeked over her shoulder to see what she was writing.

"Hurry," Mikal said. "The soldiers may come back to search us."

Lyra handed Makvar the note with a flourish. "There you are, captain." Straightening with a grunt, Mikal asked what she wrote.

"'To Excellent Imolla, high master of the Guild of Constant Working in Farhaven, kingdom of Periskold: greetings. Know that this man, Makvar, master of the barge *Four Brothers*, was promised 100 gold marks to deliver to you Orichalkon, the Sungam Smith's magical head. He was prevented by Count Rynelo, but he should be paid anyway.'"

The first star, the Wander Jewel, appeared in the eastern sky. It wasn't very dark, but boatloads of Rynelo's men were already boarding craft nearest the boom.

Makvar's men lowered a skiff from the stern. It was loaded with water, food, and two blankets.

Makvar offered Mikal a sword. It was short and thick, with a straight blade. Touched, Mikal declined. He was no warrior.

"The crossbow, then?"

Lyra vetoed that. The bow was too heavy for them to span and unwieldy to shoot. In the end, Makvar gave them a matching pair of common boatmen's knives, like all his crew carried. They clasped hands, and the children carefully climbed over the side into the skiff.

Mikal took the oars and slowly pulled away. No one on *Four Brothers* watched them go.

CHAPTER 9

Two Paws

L yra and Mikal landed on the north shore of the lake. Once they unloaded the skiff, Mikal waded out with it until the current took it away. It would do them no good for the empty boat to be found where they went ashore.

They decided to head away from the lake a few leagues before turning west for Farhaven. They had no exact idea which way to go, but Mikal believed if they stayed within a day's walk of the river and went into the setting sun, they had to reach Farhaven eventually.

Unlike the eastern provinces, western Periskold was not as hilly or as heavily wooded. They passed sizable farms and apple orchards. Periskolders in this region raised great herds of cattle, kept in by high log fences. Mikal and Lyra avoided these farms. They were guarded by fierce dogs, and the farmers did not welcome strangers.

Lyra was puzzled by the height and strength of the fences. They were cutting through an airy pine woods three days from the lake.

"Why make the fences so high?" she wondered. Pine needles were so thick underfoot that their footfalls made no sound. In the stillness, their voices sounded strange, even though they spoke quietly.

"Cows can jump," Mikal said. "I've seen calves leap a rock wall as tall as my chest."

Lyra wasn't convinced. "Why make the fences so thick? They're like the stockade at Kenvist's camp!" She looked around at the widely spaced trees and scant undergrowth. "There can't be any Fey folk around here."

Mikal agreed. The Fey folk dwelt in dense hardwood forests. The farms were too large and too numerous to allow any room for the ancient inhabitants.

The question of fences didn't worry Mikal. His feet were sore, and he was tired of walking. Sunset was not far off. It was time to find a place to rest for the night.

Since leaving Perisk's Bowl, there had been no signs of pursuit. At first, they took turns keeping watch, one of them staying awake while the other slept. It was Mikal's turn on watch tonight, and he didn't relish the idea. He wanted to sleep.

He spotted a trio of pines growing close together. Their trunks made a cozy triangle full of brown straw. This, he announced, was their bed for the night.

He set Orry on the ground facing out from the pines. Lyra scraped down to bare earth and started a small fire with flint and steel (Makvar had thought of everything). The children ate in silence as night fell around them. Overhead, tree frogs chirped and creaked. Mikal toasted a crust of bread over the fire. Lyra sipped from the water jug.

A far-off howl split the air. The jug froze halfway to Lyra's lips.

"What was that?"

Mikal wasn't sure, but right away he noticed the frogs ceased singing. Thick silence followed until they heard the howl again.

"Wolf," Orry said. Mikal's bread was charred black.

"Are there wolves in Periskold?" demanded Lyra.

"It s-seems so. I would say less than half a l-league away."

Mikal looked up. The pines were like ship's masts: tall, straight, and branchless. There was no way to climb them to hide.

He sighed. "It's my watch tonight. I'll keep the fire going." No wolf would approach a campfire.

"You are t-tired," Orry said. "Why n-not rest? I will st-stand watch."

They retreated inside the pines. Tying their blankets to the trees, the children walled themselves inside.

Mikal stuck both knives into the straw, points first. With his back against one tree and Lyra against another, they tried to settle down to sleep. The eerie silence continued. Mikal smelled the sharp, piney smoke of the campfire.

Lyra began snoring softly. The girl could sleep through a battle, he thought.

Mikal must have dozed, because the next thing he knew, Orry was saying, "Mikal, Mikal, Mikal . . . Mikal,

Mikal, Mikal." Not loudly, but his tone sent a thrill of fear through the boy. He grabbed his knife and listened.

"Mikal, Mikal, Mikal—"

"Orry, what's going on?"

"There's s-something out th-there, Mikal."

"Wolf?"

"N-not unless wolves w-walk on t-two feet."

Two feet? Mikal stood up slowly, peering over the top of the blanket. The fire was out. All around was deepest night. Orry was on the ground a step away, facing north.

"Where is it?" he whispered.

"Str-straight out my n-nose, forty p-paces."

"What's it doing?"

"L-looking at us!"

Mikal heard a rustling. Orry whispered the intruder was moving off to the right. Mikal knelt and shook Lyra.

"Wake up!" he said. "There's someone out there!"

Her eyes sprang open. "Harlano?"

It didn't feel like Harlano was near. The wizard wouldn't stalk them alone in the forest. He'd send Quintane's men to round them up.

"Maybe it's some farmer. . . ."

Mikal hissed, "In the dark of night?"

The mysterious visitor moved beyond Orry's sight. Mikal stepped over the blanket and picked him up.

"Do you see him?"

Tiny gears turned inside the bronze skull. "N-no . . ."

Mikal circled the three pines, keeping Orry's eyes on the outer darkness. He'd gone halfway around the trees when something less black than the night slammed into him. Down he went, losing Orry and his knife.

Snarling filled his face. Mikal saw a gray muzzle, black nose, and yellow teeth. He got his hands up in time to ward off the snapping jaws trying to close on his throat. The beast was big and heavy, pinning him to the ground. Held down as he was, he couldn't see anything but matted gray fur. He screamed for Lyra.

He heard her yell. Lyra leaped on the creature's back and wrapped her arms around its throat, trying to drag it away from Mikal. When that failed, she struck it hard with the butt of her knife. The beast shuddered violently and bucked, throwing Lyra off with ease.

It reared up over Mikal. In his horror, he saw the thing was standing on its hind legs. It looked like an enormous wolf, but it stood upright like a man.

Mikal scrambled backward. Orry rolled behind him. The horrible beast dropped on all fours and stalked toward him. It tried to swat Orry aside, but the bronze head did something remarkable. Having no weapons, or even hands to wield any, Orry bit the creature on its front leg. His metal jaw was fitted with bronze teeth, shaped like human teeth.

The beast grunted and stopped. Lifting its leg, it shook the metal head loose. Black liquid eyes found

Mikal cowering in the pine straw. It advanced a step, staggered, and collapsed.

Lyra was on it in a flash, knife held high—sharp end this time.

Mikal cried, "No, Lyra, wait!"

Why he said that, he never knew. The giant wolf slunk away, favoring its bitten leg. Mikal got up. Together, he and Lyra watched the monster creep off. Lyra yelled and stamped her foot, brandishing her knife. The wolf flinched, then dashed into the surrounding darkness.

Turning to Mikal, Lyra demanded, "Are you hurt? Are you bitten?"

"No."

"Let me see!"

She dragged up his shirt, searching for wounds. He pushed her away.

"I am all right," he said.

"Fate, that's good. I wouldn't want to have to cut your throat!"

Mikal put a hand to his neck. Why would she say such a thing?

"Those bitten by a werewolf become a monster, too," she said.

He thought about that. "Do you think it was a werewolf?"

"Fury, yes! Did you see it? It was twice the size of a normal wolf, and it stood up like a man!"

He spied Orry lying nose-down in the dirt. "He saved me," Mikal said.

"Huh, *I* saved you," Lyra replied.

He picked up his metallic friend. There was gray fur in Orry's teeth. Dark blood smeared his brazen lips.

"Thank you."

"Y-you're w-welcome." Orry's eyelids opened and closed with a gritty sound. Mikal brushed dirt and straw from his friend's face.

"Didn't know you were a fighter," Lyra said.

"Neither d-did I."

They retired inside the blanket walls. Lyra said in a low voice, "Now we know why the local farmers put such strong fences around their herds."

After the terror of the attack, Mikal remained awake for the rest of the night. Dawn arrived cold and gray. A chill wind blew down from the north. The children packed their things and resumed their march.

"Come night, we have to find a better place to stay," Lyra said. "A farmhouse, a barn, anything."

"Why? Do you think it will rain?" Mikal asked.

"The ch-chance of precipitation is s-sixty percent," Orry said.

"I'm not worried about rain or precipitation. That werewolf may attack again," Lyra said. Mikal asked why. "When a beast like that gets a scent in its nose, it doesn't give up until it devours its prey."

"H-how do you n-know so much about werewolves?"

"I used to go to the Theater of Terrors in Oranbold all the time."

"Sneak in, you mean," Mikal said.

Lyra ignored him. "I saw plays about creatures of the night. Werewolves never give up till they kill their prey."

"Those were plays." Mikal said. "You can't go by what's said in a play."

"Why not?"

"It's made-up, it's a story—just a tale to scare folks. What they say isn't real."

"Maybe it is!"

They argued through the whole morning. At noon, they tried to approach a woman they saw drawing water from a well. She fled, leaving her bucket behind. A short time later, they met a man driving a small herd of calves. Seeing Lyra and Mikal, he set his dogs on them. They had to run quite far to escape.

"What is wrong with people around here?" Mikal gasped after the dogs turned back.

"Afraid," Lyra puffed. "Werewolf. Could be anyone by day. Suspect strangers!"

By late afternoon, they had come to a vast open meadow. The high grass was already brown. Walking a ways, they found a heap of flat boulders. Mikal climbed up. Even on a cloudy day, the rock soaked up a nice amount of the sun's heat. He set Orry on a convenient ledge and stretched out. Wearily, Lyra joined them. Orry began to sing.

"Not too loud," Lyra said. "I'm too tired to run from another pack of dogs."

It was pleasant up there in the cool air with a warm stone to lie on. Orry sang one ditty after another. Oddly, he didn't stutter while singing. Comfortable, Mikal fell asleep. He had precious little rest the night before.

Sometime later, a shadow fell across his face. His senses, keen from being chased so long, woke him from a sound slumber.

Crouching on the gray stone was a woman. She was lean and sun-browned, with wild, tangled hair the color of the clouds. Her feet were bare. All she wore were a few scraps of leather. On her left forearm was a bandage of tightly wrapped vines and leaves.

"Who are you?" Mikal managed to say. The woman stared at him. Her expression was more curious than threatening, but her appearance was so strange that Mikal felt a powerful urge to flee.

"Lyra . . ." The girl was snoring a few steps away. "Lyra!"

She rolled over, complaining in her sleep. Mikal said, "Orry? Orry!"

"The head cannot speak." The woman's voice was quite low, but not unappealing. "I stopped him."

Mikal glanced at his friend. Orry's eyes were wide and round. A thick piece of tree limb was jammed in his mouth.

"Who are you?"

"Killeen."

"What do you want?"

She uncoiled with grace and ease.

"I come to serve you," she said.

"Serve me? Why?"

"You have undone a great evil that was done to me."

Mikal was completely confused. What evil, and how had he undone anything?

Killeen held up her leaf-bandaged arm. "By your power, my curse is undone—in part."

The truth hit him like a thunderbolt.

"You're the wolf!"

She folded her arms and nodded. "I am. For six and twenty years I have held this province in fear. Last night, that fear was banished." He asked how.

Killeen looked surprised. "Know you not? Your talisman, your making of power, shed my blood. By this I am cured of my lust for killing."

Gradually, Mikal came to understand what Killeen meant. When Orry bit her, somehow the spell that compelled Killeen to kill was broken.

"You're welcome," Lyra said, rubbing her eyes. She awakened in time to hear the last of Killeen's story.

"I am glad you are freed," Mikal said. He swallowed and found it hard. "Fate go with you in your life, Killeen!"

She shook her head

"My fate is to follow you, young wizard. To the end of the world, if need be."

CHAPTER 10

Six Days, Six Nights

"Why does she have to follow us?" Lyra said in a not-too-soft whisper. Killeen was trailing them by half a dozen steps. Joining the children on their trek, she remained at their heels, never leading.

"She feels honor-bound," Mikal replied as quietly as he could.

They had left the piney uplands behind them, descending to the bottom land on the north shore of the Tombow River. Compared to the wild and rocky river of the deep forest, here the Tombow was wide and peaceful. Boats and barges glided up and downstream, laden with trade. Timber, furs, cattle, and leather went downstream to Farhaven. Metal, pottery, and finished cloth flowed the other way.

So far Killeen had been a perfect companion. She spoke little, demanded nothing, trotting behind them like a faithful dog. The one thing she would not do was carry Orry. Lyra tried to pass the bronze head off on her, but she stood back, hands tight against her sides.

She seemed afraid she might somehow regain her curse if she touched him.

The first night Killeen passed with Mikal and Lyra revealed how much of her curse had been removed. Shortly before sunset, she laid a campfire for the children, and then departed into a nearby thicket. A short time later, she emerged in wolf form. Lyra took to her heels, running and yelling as hard as she could. Mikal would have run too, but before he could, Killeen came and lay at his feet. Trembling, he dared to pat her dusty gray head. The fearsome wolf licked his hand.

Killeen's uncontrollable desire to kill was gone, but she still changed into a wolf each night. At dawn, she left again and returned as a woman.

"How did you come to be a werewolf?" Lyra asked bluntly that first morning.

"It is the curse of a wizard," Killeen said. "When I was but ten years old, my father ran afoul of a sorcerer named Verjilon. They had a dispute about some rare herbs my father collected for him. My father accused Verjilon of trying to cheat him. The wizard claimed my father kept gold for himself and supplied the wrong herbs he needed for a conjuration. Verjilon's great patron, the Queen Mother of Darland, threw the wizard into the dungeon of Castle Morthret. From there, Verjilon cursed my entire family."

"Did you all become werewolves?" Mikal asked.

"No, only I. In a dream, the sorcerer told me the only way to end my curse was for me to kill my father. This I would not do. I ran away, as far as my legs would carry me. I have been in Periskold for six and twenty years."

Killeen had haunted the pine lands, killing cattle and the occasional hunter who tried to catch her. All attempts to capture or kill the werewolf had failed. The farmers tried to appease her by offering sacrificial cows, but they never understood the nature of Killeen's curse. She had to stalk and kill her prey. Nothing else would satisfy the dark curse Verjilon had placed on her.

Privately, Mikal asked Orry, "How did you change her just by a bite?"

"I d-do not know," he confessed. "I f-feared for your life and bit the beast. I had n-no idea it would af-f-fect her this w-way."

In the end, Mikal offered to take Killeen's case to Excellent Imolla. If anyone could banish her full curse, she could.

Five days they walked after Killeen joined them. In five days, they came within sight of the walls of Farhaven. The city was huge, much larger than Oranbold or Woodhaven. Leagues away they could see the spires of tall towers, yellow stone walls, and a haze of chimney smoke hanging over the city. They were out of provisions and had little money left. Lyra suggested they find a likely tavern and set themselves up as soothsayers again.

Orry could make them some money, and then they could go see the Guild mistress in style.

"We don't have time for that. Fate only knows where Harlano is. If he followed the river, he could have reached Farhaven ahead of us," Mikal said. He could be poisoning Imolla's ear even now.

They were perched on a low bluff overlooking the river. Below, a well-traveled road bordered the river.

"Food. We need food," Lyra said.

"Master, please allow me to get the things you need," Killeen said.

"No!" Mikal, Lyra, and Orry said together. Killeen was puzzled by their loud agreement.

"We do not want you killing or robbing anyone," Lyra said.

Killeen shrugged. She squatted on a log overlooking the road on her haunches, looking very wolf-like even in her human skin.

She raised her head, sniffing the wind. "I smell meat."

Lyra looked alarmed, but Mikal smelled it, too. Smoke borne on the wind brought with it the tang of roasting flesh. There must be a camp or roadside tavern below.

Carefully slipping Orry into a blanket-cloth bag, Mikal said they should find food first. If the company was friendly, they might find out how best to reach Excellent Imolla once inside Farhaven.

On the road they attracted many stares. They were an odd trio: scruffy, dirty Lyra, with a big sailor's knife thrust through the sash around her waist; Mikal, grown tall and gawky, dressed in a mismatch of clothing from the Miracle Fair, the Guild house in Woodhaven, and Makvar's generous leavings. Strangest of all was Killeen. She had cleaned up a bit since becoming human, but she still looked like a wild woman of the woods, clad in scraps of leather and tanned like a boot. A few travelers snickered or made comments in passing. Lyra glowered at them, fingering the hilt of her knife. Mikal feared she would cause more trouble than Killeen.

They found the source of the delicious scent of roasting meat. A sprawling inn filled a bend in the road. Built of great logs, it had a huge central chimney and wide porches facing the road. Mikal, Lyra, and Killeen went to the horse trough and carefully washed their hands and faces.

Single horses were tied up to hitching posts along the porch. Wagons laden with trade goods filled the yard behind the horses. Each wagon was watched over by a guard or fierce dog. The dogs stood quivering atop their carts, nearly crazed by Killeen. She glared back at them, eyes narrow, nostrils flaring.

"I hate dogs," she muttered.

Mikal linked his arm in hers. "Now, now, come inside. You're a person again. People don't need to fight with dogs."

Near the main door was a fine coach. The four matched chestnut horses whinnied and stamped when Killeen passed. She paused to smile at them, and they went berserk. The coachman had to come out of the inn to calm his team. Mikal made note of Killeen's effect on animals. It might be useful.

The inn's common room was a wide, smoky place, forested with wooden posts and worn tables, crowded with noisy, feasting travelers. A steward with a white apron spotted them.

"Tramps outside!" he said above the din. Lyra held up her purse and shook it significantly. The steward shrugged and stepped aside. He didn't know Lyra's purse was filled with shells and pebbles.

They found room at the end of a long table near the fire. Two enormous iron spits stood before the flames. One held an entire pig, the other a side of beef. Killeen gazed at the roasting meat longingly.

"How much do you have left?" Lyra murmured in Mikal's ear.

He checked. "Just two silver crowns and a brass cartwheel."

On the soot-blackened stones over the fireplace the innkeeper had chalked a curly-cue, followed by "0–4–0". This meant a serving of pork cost four silver crowns. Next to it was marked a pair of longhorns and the numbers "0–5–5." Beef cost five silver crowns, five cartwheels. High prices, but they were outside a big city.

Mikal said cheerfully, "Bread is one silver a loaf! We can get two!" The girl and woman were not amused.

Men at the far end of the table roared with delight. They were arm-wrestling, and one fellow had beaten his opponent after a hard struggle. Lyra watched many coins change hands after the bout. She grinned. Leaning across, she whispered in Killeen's ear. Slowly the wolf woman nodded.

"C'mon," she told Mikal. He picked up Orry's bag and followed, unsure what Lyra was up to.

"Ho, friends!" she hailed the men. They were brawny, rough types, wagon drivers by the look of them. "Who won the wrestling match?"

A dark man with a pointed, black beard growled, "I did. Why?"

"Want another match?"

His companion guffawed. "Against you, little girl?"

"No, my sister here." Killeen put her hands on her hips and smiled with surprising winsomeness.

The drivers almost fell off their benches laughing. They called Killeen all sorts of rough names, of which "scarecrow" was the kindest. Lyra scowled.

"Twenty gold crowns says my sister can beat Spade-face, here!" She pointed a thumb at the winner of the last contest. Behind his black beard, the man reddened.

"Have you got twenty crowns?" he said. Again Lyra jingled her purse as proof. Mikal's heart hammered.

If the wagoneers demanded to see the color of her money, they would surely get beaten for their audacity.

"She's serious," said one of the other men.

"Do it, Rendal! Twenty crowns will buy us a night in Farhaven we'll never forget!" cried another.

The wagoneers collected the equivalent of twenty gold crowns in silver and brass. This was piled on the table next to Lyra's pebble-filled purse.

Spade-face (Rendal, apparently) grandly gestured for Killeen to sit down. She did, examining the bench and table with obvious curiosity. Mikal feared she would say something that would give her true nature away, but she said not a word but took her place.

"Tavern rules," said Spade-face. "Lift your elbow off the table, and you lose. No kicking under the table, or spitting in your opponent's eye." Killeen nodded at these sensible rules.

"Other than that," he went on, grinning, "all's fair!"

"Right hand or left?" Killeen asked.

"Right."

They clamped their hands together. Spade-face weighed twice as much as Killeen. His shoulders looked as wide as Lyra was tall. Mikal closed his eyes. There was no Kenvist or Makvar to help them here. When Lyra's scheme failed, they were due for a thrashing.

"Go!" shouted Spade-face's friend. He tensed his arm, trying to throw Killeen quickly. Her arm did not budge. Surprised, the wagon driver pushed even harder.

Mikal saw the tendons in Killeen's neck tighten. However, she remained unmovable.

Spade-face gripped the edge of the table with his left hand for better leverage. He leaned into his push, grunting. Killeen's left hand was lying in her lap.

The men began to mutter and swear under their breath. Mikal counted how many steps it would take to reach the inn door.

"Push back, why don't you?" Spade-face sputtered. "What are you made of, oak?"

"No kicking, no spitting, yes?" said Killeen.

"That's—right—!"

"What about butting?"

Spade-face did not understand in time. He looked up, wondering, just in time for Killeen to smash her forehead into his. He flew back. She held onto his hand and pressed it to the table with a solid thump. When she let go, he slid sideways, disappearing under the table.

Silence. Killeen picked up a handy mug and drained it. "Good cider," she said.

Lyra scraped the wager into her hands. It was too much for her to hold, so she called Mikal to help. He did, under the furious stares of the wagon drivers.

"Who are you?" one demanded. To Killeen he added, "*What* are you?"

"Hungry travelers," Lyra declared.

"This smells wrong. It's a cheat. What are you, wizards?"

"What, two children and a vagabond?" said Mikal, trying to laugh. His short chuckle drew a muffled response from Orry inside his bag.

"What was that?"

"Nothing. Me. I laughed," Mikal said.

A meaty hand snatched the bag from his hands. "Heavy," said the wagoneer. "What is it, a magic crystal? Some sort of luck talisman?"

"Why don't you look and see?" Killeen said.

Mikal tried to stop him, but the men brushed him aside. The teamster set Orry on the table and skinned away the bag.

Orry opened his eyes and said, "Heh-heh-hello!"

"Magic! It was a cheat! Get them!"

The men kicked over their benches and stood in a circle around Lyra, Mikal, and Killeen.

"Where is the justice in this?" Lyra demanded. "All of you against just us!"

"Shall I kill them?" Killeen asked quietly.

"No, no, don't do that!" Mikal pleaded.

The nearest man threw a punch at the wolf-woman. She dodged neatly and let him stumble away, upset by his own momentum. Another man tried to grab her from behind, pinning her arms. Killeen broke his hold with ease, turned, and flattened him with a sharp blow to the chin. Someone took Lyra by the collar. She screamed as if she were being murdered.

That set off the entire room. People crowded forward to see what the trouble was. Others, no doubt with trouble of their own, quietly made for the doors.

A hard-fisted wagon driver seized Mikal by his shirt. Orry bellowed in the voice he used to command the crew of the *Four Brothers*: "Unhand him, you knave!" Startled, the man did just that. Mikal dropped to the floor and crawled under the table.

Killeen had knocked down four men, not including Spade-face. New challengers kept coming, whooping and yelling, leaping from tables. She dodged a few, hurled others to the floor, and kept her head while everyone around her seemed to be going crazy.

Down at the floor, Lyra struck savagely at any feet and ankles that came within reach. She was buried under a sprawl of bodies. Mikal pulled her out. She had a tuft of something brown in her teeth.

"Is that cloth?"

Lyra spit it out. "Beard," she said. "Get Orry and let's be gone!"

"Right." She pushed him out from under the table. At first, he protested, but he saw Orry on the table, shouting encouragement to the brawlers around him. Through a gap in the fighting Mikal darted in, grabbed Orry, and ducked back under the table.

"Where's Killeen?"

"Up there somewhere!"

Mikal said, "We must help her—" A clay jug smashed in front of them. Close behind fell a patron, soaked with cider and bleeding from the nose.

"I don't think she needs much help," Lyra said.

Through the chaos they heard the peal of a trumpet. It sounded again, *ta-ra-ra, ta-ra-ra*. Its effect on the brawlers was almost magical. Punches paused in mid-throw, throttling ceased, and broken mugs fell to the floor, shattering.

"The Watch! The Watch!"

Being a sizable city, Farhaven had a public watch battalion whose job it was to keep order. Evidently, they were good at it. The inn's common room began to empty like a washtub with a big hole in the bottom.

Strong hands dragged Mikal out from under the table. It was Killeen.

"Stand here," she said. He did. She pulled Lyra out by the feet even though the girl clung to the table leg, trying to kick loose. When she saw Killeen had her, Lyra jumped to her feet.

"Time to go—!"

"No."

Killeen had a black eye, and her lower lip was puffed up sausage-size.

"Why don't we get out before the Watch arrives?" Mikal asked.

"You want to meet the wizard Imolla, don't you?"

He was impressed with her wisdom. What surer way could they get the attention of Excellent Imolla than by being taken to her by the City Watch?

The front doors burst open. A double line of men in steel helmets rushed in and fanned out. Some brawlers resisted and were quickly subdued.

In came a tall man, dark-skinned, with a plume on his helmet. The Watch stood at attention when he entered. There was no one else in the whole inn standing but Killeen, Mikal, and Lyra. The officer approached.

"What's all this?" he said in a vast, deep voice.

"The fight is nothing," Killeen replied. She pointed at Orry. "We must see Excellent Imolla at once. Will you take us to her?"

Orry added with a click of his brazen eyelids, "It's a m-matter of gr-grave importance!"

If the watch commander was surprised at being addressed by a metal head, he did not show it. Turning to his men he said, "Form ranks! Escort these people to the Guild hall!"

Mikal blinked. Sometimes, things were simple.

CHAPTER II

TWO JOBS

The Watch marched them through the streets of Farhaven. Mikal felt like a prisoner walking in the midst of so many soldiers. Lyra enjoyed it. She mimicked the guards' pace, swinging her arms in time with their cadence. Ahead, Killeen urged them on. At first, Mikal did not understand what the hurry was. Mikal finally realized why: It was late afternoon. At sunset, Killeen would revert to wolf shape. It wouldn't do for this to happen before the children had a chance to explain her unusual condition.

Farhaven was not too different from Oranbold, the capital of Phalia, though much larger. Houses were chiefly wood, three or four stories high. The street was neatly paved with red brick. There were more word signs around; that meant more people could read. People were more varied than in Phalia, too. Mikal saw many dark-skinned folk, like the captain of the Watch. Orry said they came from the islands west of Florian. Florians were there in their short kilts, along with Periskolders in furs from the eastern woodlands, and many barefoot

Darlanders in chaps and vests. Mikal enjoyed looking around until he saw someone he knew.

He grabbed Lyra's wrist. "Quintane!" he hissed. The mercenary's face hardened when his eyes met Mikal's.

Lyra saw him, too. She called him an ugly word.

"If he's here, Harlano cannot be far," Mikal said.

Killeen doubled back between the marching files of Watchmen and pushed the children along. "Move swiftly, please! The day grows short."

They reached a second wall slicing through the city. Built of giant blocks of stone, it looked much older than the outer defense. Soldiers on the gate saluted as the plumed officer led his men through. Inside the inner wall, the city was very different. The buildings were taller, older, darker, and more cramped. Streets narrowed until walking three abreast became impossible.

Mikal looked up at the dark overhanging houses. He smelled a hundred suppers simmering. His belly growled so loudly that he had to cinch his belt tighter to stop it. Too bad the fight in the inn happened before they ate.

"My lord, where are we bound?" Killeen asked the officer.

"To the Magister's Hall."

"Is it far?"

"See that dome, yonder? That's it."

Above the twisting lanes and timeworn dwellings loomed a massive domed building of pale gray stone. Mikal was studying it when Lyra snatched at his sleeve.

"Smell that? It's the sea!" she said.

If that's what the sea smelled like, it needed cleaning. Moldy, salty, kind of rotten—that's how Mikal would have described what he smelled. He had never been near the sea before. He didn't feel like he had missed anything.

Instead of a great square or ceremonial plaza, the Magister's Hall rose up in the forest of houses like a monstrous mushroom. The street widened a bit as it circled the great dome, but it was no wider than two horses. Mikal asked the Watch officer why things were so cramped in Farhaven.

"It's an old city," he said. "Parts of the port and the Old Town go back a thousand years." As the city grew, houses sprouted around the Guild hall until the mighty building was surrounded.

The watch battalion halted in unison, the heel of each guard's right foot striking the pavement at the same time. Killeen and the children stopped, too. When no one said anything, the wolf-woman walked ahead a few paces and turned back.

"What now?"

"If you are seeing Excellent Imolla, you must continue on your own," said the officer. "We may not enter beyond this point."

Mikal understood. "There's a magical line," he said to his companions. "Soldiers cannot cross it."

He strode ahead, half expecting to sense some sort of magical barrier. He felt nothing. Lyra and Killeen followed without any problem.

The Watch commander raised his sword in salute.

"When you see our esteemed, Excellent Imolla, please tell her Watch Battalion Number Five delivered you. Captain Razhir, commanding."

Mikal swore he would give them proper credit. Waving good-bye, he trailed Lyra and Killeen into the massive hall.

At street level, the hall was surrounded by a deep colonnade made of hundreds and hundreds of gray stone pillars. Up close they were wavy and bumpy looking. Lyra ran her hand over one.

"Carving," she said, "almost worn away."

They walked on. It soon became clear something unnatural was happening. Though they walked and walked straight ahead, they never seemed to get any farther into the building.

"Let's go this way," Lyra suggested, pointing to her left. Mikal asked why.

"Why not?"

She set off. Killeen shrugged and went, too. Lugging Orry, Mikal trailed after them.

They walked long enough to have circled the great domed building, and still no entrance was plain.

"There is a spell on the entrance," Mikal said. To Orry he added, "What do you think?"

"An old and d-dark edi-f-fice. Wrapped in old, d-dark spells."

"How do we get in?" wondered Lyra.

Just then Mikal noticed Killeen was gone. He spun around, but the wolf-woman was not in sight. Behind them, the street outside the Magister's Hall had grown dim. The sun had set.

Killeen glided in like a ghost, gray fur and padded paws. She nuzzled Mikal's hand reassuringly, then loped away into the shadows.

"F-follow the lycan-th-thrope," Orry said. "A wolf can see things humans cannot."

Lyra and Mikal kept Killeen in view. She seemed to go straight ahead a ways, then turned abruptly right. When they caught up with her, she was staring into black space, ears laid back and tail drooping.

"Is it safe?" whispered Mikal.

In answer, Killeen bounded ahead. All at once they saw a dim opening in the darkness, a great open arch. They drew nearer, and a flaming torch appeared in a sconce over the arch.

"The way in?" Mikal held Orry tight. Lyra fingered her knife. Across the width of the entrance, Killeen sniffed the stone floor. Satisfied, she went in. The children kept close behind.

They passed along a wide tunnel. There were no doors or decoration, just gray stone walls, ceiling, and floor. Every so often they came to a blazing torch in an iron bracket. On impulse, Mikal touched the bottom of one sconce. The metal should have been hot. It wasn't. To Mikal, it felt as cold as the stone walls around them.

The fire was not real. Could they find the true way in? Between Killeen's wolf senses and Orry's insights, they ought to be able to penetrate most ordinary deceptions—or so Mikal hoped.

"Is it me, or is the floor slanting up?" Lyra said.

Orry replied, "The f-floor is indeed sl-slanting up at four and a half d-degrees."

Now that they mentioned it, Mikal could feel it, too. Killeen galloped ahead. She passed out of sight. Mikal walked faster. Lyra complained he was rushing into danger, but she hurried after him. Better together than apart in a weird place like this.

Mikal emerged at the top of the ramp in a vast columned hall. Indifferently lit, the air was cool and dry. Torches stacked on iron trees flanked the ends of the ramp. A few paces away, two more burning trees stood, and another pair beyond them.

"Hello?" called Mikal. Lyra elbowed him in the gut.

"Are you trying to get us killed?"

"We're supposed to be here," he reminded her. "Excellent Imolla is a just and wise wizard, everybody says."

"Everybody's not with us now."

"Th-there!" They saw Killeen standing by the third pair of torch-trees.

"Notice something?" Mikal said as they went to join Killeen.

"What?"

"Where are the apprentices? Where are the Gleanings?" The Guild hall in Oranbold had been like an ants' nest, filled with hundreds of children and youths busy doing the work of the master wizards. The ancient Magister's Hall was like a tomb. Were there no new magicians being trained in Farhaven?

Where Killeen stood there was an open space in the columns. They followed the wolf-woman into a brighter circle of light. Wedged between two thick stone pillars was a grand table, heaped with scrolls, books, and documents. Seated at the table was a solitary scribe, busily scratching away with a long goose quill pen.

Lyra cleared her throat.

"I know you're there," said the scribe. Dwarfed by heaps of loose scrolls, it was hard to tell what the scribe looked like. Mikal had an impression of dark hair and a dusty brown robe.

Killeen panted. The scribe finished a page, pushed it aside, and started another.

"Tell your werewolf to be quiet."

"Tell her yourself," Lyra said.

"Begging your pardon." Mikal broke in before Lyra said something regrettable. "We are here to see the wizard Imolla."

"Excellent Imolla," said Lyra. Killeen whined and sat down on her haunches.

"I can tell I will get no more work done until you are gone," said the scribe. "Come forward to the light."

They stood in line at the table: Mikal, with Orry; Killeen, and Lyra. This close, Mikal saw that the scribe was a woman of middle years, plump and pale. Her chestnut hair was streaked with gray. Her eyes were golden brown and bloodshot.

"What a strange band of visitors," she said, putting down her pen. "A boy with a null aura, an automaton head, a werewolf, and the scruffiest girl-child in Periskold."

"Null aura? What's that?" Lyra said. Mikal wondered too, but there were more pressing matters to discuss.

Mikal set Orry on the table. "This is Orichalkon. He was made by Sungam the Smith—"

"Yes, I know. A very special artifact. Where did you get it?"

He explained how he was gleaned in Phalia. Taken to the Guild of Constant Working in Oranbold, there he was apprenticed to Master Harlano. Mikal found Orry in Master Harlano's rooms, lifeless. He discovered Orry drew power from sunlight. When Harlano disobeyed the will of his Guild masters and started a war with Darland, Mikal, Lyra, and Orry fled when Harlano burned the Guild hall to the ground.

For two years, the children and the bronze head wandered from Phalia to Periskold. They cleaned stables, picked crops, and once shoveled coal at an ironmongery. For almost a year, they lived on the edge of complete poverty, then found Anglebart and the Miracle Fair. That relatively comfortable life came to an abrupt end when Harlano found them again.

"You're only telling her about the good times," Lyra said. "Tell her about the bad days, too." Mikal pointedly ignored her.

The scribe nodded. "And the werewolf? I've never seen a tame one in all my years."

Lyra jumped in and told the tale of Killeen attacking them, only to be driven off by Lyra's terrible dagger thrusts, and a bite from Orry. It wasn't exactly the truth, but it was close for Lyra. Killeen was cured of her thirst for killing, but not cured of her shape-shifting.

"Now you're on the run," the scribe said, rising to her feet. She wasn't very tall, only a little more than Mikal. "Harlano pursues you?"

"Yes, lady. He has chased us across all of Periskold," Mikal said.

The plump little scribe rolled up a parchment into a tight tube. She sealed it with ribbon and wax, and with an upward toss, the scroll vanished.

"Harlano is indeed in Farhaven. I knew not why. I have just dispatched a warning to the Guild masters in other lands."

Killeen whined in her throat. Lyra patted her and told her to be quiet.

"We hoped Excellent Imolla could help us—protect us—against Harlano. We've managed to escape several times, but he won't give up!" Mikal said.

"She cannot do much to help you," said the scribe. Lyra demanded to know why. The woman gestured around them.

"I am alone here. Since Harlano's treachery came to light, many wizards, masters and apprentices, have gone forth to find him. None have returned. Many are dead or petrified. A few even joined Harlano. Imolla can defend the Magister's Hall, but little more."

She came out from behind the broad table. Mikal saw the lightning pendant around her neck. He bowed. Killeen lowered her chin to the floor. Lyra was perplexed.

"What's this?" she said.

"Don't you know who this is?"

Lyra didn't, so the scribe said, "I am Imolla, called the Excellent. As of this time and place, I am also the last wizard of Farhaven."

CHAPTER 12

THREE ESCAPE

Imolla took her guests deeper into the Magister's Hall. She ignited torches with waves of her hand as they followed long passages into the heart of the ancient building. Along the way, she related bits of the history of the hall and the Guild of Constant Working in Farhaven.

"This is the second oldest Guild hall in the world," she said. "Only the Conjurer's Keep, in Wenzeland, is older."

Mikal didn't know that. He had never heard of Wenzeland.

"The great sage Miraco the Mason created the hall himself, using only magic. The effort killed him. His body now rests in a black stone sarcophagus under the great dome."

"Was this during the time of Sungam the Smith?" Mikal asked.

Imolla glanced back. "Why, yes. How did you know?"

"A guess." During his time as Harlano's apprentice, Mikal had to read histories of the wizards' order. In Sungam's time, master wizards always had a sobriquet, or nickname: Sungam the Smith, Rainmaker Armeen, and so on. It made sense a magician known as Miraco the Mason lived at the same time.

Imolla took them to a surprisingly normal kitchen somewhere deep in the hall. There, over a smoky brazier, Lyra and Mikal finally made themselves a meal. Mikal tossed roasted bits of beef to Killeen, who lay quietly in the corner. Lyra ate like a shipwreck survivor. Using both hands, she gorged on fruit preserves, smoked chicken, pickles, and a kind of salty, powdered cheese. When the bread ran out, she hunted among the shelves for more.

Mikal said, "Do you know why Harlano wants Orichalkon so badly?"

Imolla poured spring water from a stone jug into Mikal's cup.

"It is a font of much knowledge."

"Orry knows where the Brightstone is."

The heavy jug smashed on the floor. Killeen bolted to her feet. Lyra peeked around a tall shelf, mouth stuffed with biscuit.

"Is that true?" Imolla asked, pale face gone even paler.

Mikal nodded. "Harlano thinks so."

"If that's true . . . " She looked at the metal head sitting on the flour-dusted table. Her expression was grim and her intention plain.

"You can't destroy Orry!" Mikal cried.

"Better to destroy him than allow Harlano to find the source of all magic!"

Lyra and Killeen returned to the table. Their curiosity was plain. Imolla rested her brow on her hands.

"You do not understand what is at stake. Harlano is not acting alone." Lyra and Mikal said nothing. "He is part of a secret society, called 'the Anvil.' Their goal is to remove all magic from the world!"

"But old baldy is a wizard! Why would he want to get rid of magic?" Lyra said.

Mikal explained that five centuries ago there had been no magic. Warlords and pretenders of secret knowledge ruled petty states usually no larger than a city and its walls. War was constant. So was suffering.

One day, without warning, the Brightstone fell from the sky. With it came magic. Wise men and women learned to use the power to help people. With their aid, half a dozen great lords established true kingdoms for the first time. The rule of law replaced rule by axe and sword. Brutal warlords and false sages had to submit to the new order or face destruction. Harlano and his fellow fanatics wanted to overthrow the Guild and bring back the rule of Might.

"But why?" Lyra wondered.

"Membership in the Anvil is closely guarded," Imolla said. "It is easy to imagine who might fill its ranks—powerless lesser lords, rich merchants with pretenses of nobility, false prophets, and failed wizards—anyone with a grudge against the current order who thinks they will gain power if true magic is destroyed."

"Do you know where the Brightstone is?" Lyra asked.

"No." Imolla folded her arms tightly. "If I did know, I would leap from a high place and keep the knowledge safe!"

"What can we do?" Mikal wondered.

"I will protect you all I can," Imolla promised, "but a greater power than mine is needed. The Anvil is everywhere. I fear Sungam's great artifact must be silenced—forever."

Mikal threw his arms around Orry. "No!"

He backed away. Imolla watched him sadly. She began to move her fingers, starting a spell. Just as Mikal was about to bolt for freedom, Orry spoke for himself.

"Magister," he said, "might I b-be altered to k-keep the secret from c-coming out?"

The fingers stopped. "Altered?"

"Yes, have my store of n-knowledge changed. F-facts deleted."

Imolla slowly dropped her hands to her sides. "Why not? Come here, boy. Bring the artifact."

Mikal didn't want to. Lyra gave him a shove. Imolla took Orry and set him on the table. She probed the back and base of his metal skull.

Orry giggled. "Your fingers are c-cold!"

"Where did he get this stutter?" she asked. Mikal told Imolla about the flume, the log, and Orry's long fall into the Tombow River.

"By Fury! No wonder he's dented."

Imolla found a hidden catch on Orry's base. There was a click, and she removed the rear half of Orry's skull. Everyone crowded in to see.

Inside the bronze shell was a mass of gears, wheels, and shiny metal orbs, all turning at different speeds and in different directions. The most arresting of these parts was a gold colored sphere a little smaller than Lyra's fist. It was etched with many fine lines running at right angles to each other. Mikal squinted hard. The lines were actually tiny notches. Fine gear teeth engaged these notches, turning—or being turned by—the golden sphere.

"What d-does it look like?" Orry asked.

"Don't you know?" answered Imolla.

"Who ever sees the back of their own head?"

Lyra launched into vivid description, full of things, bits, do-littles and do-lots. Fascinated by the works, Mikal gingerly touched a fingertip to a large cogwheel.

"Ehh? What'sss thaaaat?" Orry's voice dropped down low and slowed to a drawl.

"Sorry!"

"Artifacts are not my field," Imolla said. "My specialty is fluid magic, Farhaven being a port city served by a river, you know." She suddenly broke into a broad smile.

"The greatest living sage of artifacts is Petruvo! If anyone can alter Sungam the Smith's work, it is he!"

"Well, collect him and let it be done!" declared Lyra.

Imolla's smile faded. "He does not live in Farhaven. He has a stronghold on the north coast, called Tormentall. We will go there."

"You will leave Farhaven?"

"For a short time. The Anvil will not trouble the city if the thing they want is not here."

"Tormentall is far."

Everyone turned to see Killeen, now a woman again. She towered over the stocky sorceress. Outside the massive Guild hall, the sun must have risen. They had passed the whole night with Excellent Imolla.

"Fear not," Imolla said. "We shall not walk there. We shall fly."

Mikal found this exciting. Lyra and Killeen did not have much to say about the prospect. Imolla excused herself to make preparations.

"Hello?" Orry called. "Huh-hello! Can someone p-put my head back tog-gether, please?"

Mikal studied the curved panel. The secret catches clicked when he pressed the bronze shell in place.

Though it was morning, Lyra and Mikal were deeply tired. Lyra curled up under the pantry table and soon was snoring happily. Unable to bear the noise, Mikal decided to find someplace quieter to rest. Killeen went with him.

Whether it was the change of hours, or the fact that Imolla had become their friend, the ancient hall had taken on a new character. The building had seemed so empty last night. Now, as the boy and the wolf-woman wandered its silent corridors, they saw it was in fact crammed with the stuff of ages.

Slim beams of sunlight pierced the interior. Motes of dust drifted through these narrow curtains. As they passed through them, one after another, they saw alcoves and stairwells filled with boxes and clay jars as tall as Lyra. The box lids were often ajar, spilling their contents on the floor. Most were filled with dusty manuscripts, scrolls, and books. Five hundred years the Guild had occupied Magister's Hall. Five hundred years of writing crowded the hallways.

Besides documents, they saw figurines, tools, and strange small bottles of colored glass. Killeen picked up one. It was dog-shaped, made of brown glass. The stopper in the middle of the figure's back had long ago decayed to dust. Nothing remained. Mikal picked up a red vial shaped like two circles touching edge to edge. Something liquid sloshed inside. When he tipped it side to side, sparkles of light shone inside. Hastily, he set it down.

He found a monumental staircase. The marble steps were worn hollow by footsteps through the ages. Mikal climbed the steps. For some reason he chose to move quietly, as if trying not to disturb scholars at work.

He emerged under the great dome. It was the biggest room he had ever seen. Mikal felt he could have put the entire Guild hall of Oranbold inside this one room. Looking up, he saw the dome was not a solid, single piece, but was made of many blocks of stone, neatly fitted together. The artistry of Miraco the Mason was amazing, but after five hundred years, some gaps had developed. Sunlight squeezed through every tiny crack, giving the illusion the dome was home to a cloud of brilliant pinpoint lights.

The rotunda was perfectly circular. Mikal spotted two more stairwells opening into the room. The most obvious feature in the room was a massive black granite wedge, off by itself.

Killeen tucked her hands under her arms. Gazing upward she said, "All this was made by one man?"

"So Imolla says," Mikal replied, barely above a whisper.

They approached the black wedge. It was fashioned from a single block of black granite, many times Mikal's height. On the slope were carved some Caddian letters and numbers. They read:

> N S M C R M
> S H T T L B
> 105
> T T S R Y
> B L L H S
> N W N K

"What does it mean?"

Mikal frowned. "I don't know."

A loud clang echoed through the dome. It didn't worry Mikal, but Killeen dropped to a crouch and narrowed her eyes.

"Something is wrong," she muttered. "That was steel striking stone!"

"Probably just Imolla, bumping around."

"Imolla is not in the hall."

Killeen's senses were keener than ordinary humans' were, even when she wasn't in wolf form. She knew people by smell, and if she said Imolla wasn't in the hall, he believed it.

"What—?" he began, but Killeen put a finger to his lips to silence him.

"Stay here. I will find out."

She sprinted to the stairs—not the one they used to get there, but the farthest ones. The sound had come from there. Killeen disappeared down the steps. Mikal waited, alert and listening.

Not ten heartbeats later, the wolf-woman reappeared, running hard at him.

"Flee!" she cried.

Out of the open stairwell came a swarm of small flying creatures. Each one glowed brightly and carried with it an odor of scalding metal, a smell Mikal knew well from his days at his father's forge. The creatures spread in a cloud behind Killeen, tiny wings flapping.

They looked like butterflies—if butterflies were made of red-hot iron.

Killeen tore past, grabbed his arm, and snatched Mikal off his feet. She tucked him under one arm and made a beeline for the closest open stairs. The swarm of burning flies spread out on either side of them. One alighted on Mikal's leg. He yelped and tried to swat it. The fiercely glowing creature took wing. Where it touched him, a long red blister welled up.

The fiery flies encircled them. Killeen skidded to a stop on the smooth marble floor. She went down on one knee, covering Mikal with her arms. They were covered with narrow red burns.

"Do not look, master. I will keep them off as long as I can!"

Having caught them, the creatures did not close in. They circled, some left, some right, keeping Killeen and Mikal trapped. When the wolf-woman lunged one way, they flew at her face until she kept still again.

"Do not test them. You will die in terrible agony, I promise. Not even a lycanthrope can bear the touch of the lava flies."

Harlano had come into the rotunda, trailed by Quintane and a dozen men. The men were armed with swords and bucklers, but they kept well back, behind their leader.

"It's been a merry chase. Now it's done. I want Orichalkon, at once."

"Fury take you!"

At the wizard's nod, three lava flies darted in, leaving searing burns on Mikal's leg, arm, and neck. Killeen smashed one to the floor with her open hand, grounding it to bits with her bare foot.

Quintane's men muttered. Their leader laughed shortly.

"Tough, aren't you? Too bad we can't try ourselves face to face!"

Killeen lifted her foot, revealing cinders on the floor and a bleeding wound on her sole.

"Any time you want to die, ask me," she replied.

"Enough! Where is the head, boy?"

"Imolla has it!" Mikal said. "Why don't you try to take it from her?"

Harlano sent his men after the wizard of Farhaven. Half of Quintane's men went down one stairwell; Quintane and the rest down the other. Before he left, the mercenary offered Harlano his sword, in case Killeen escaped the circle of lava flies.

"I do not need it," the wizard said mildly. "Go."

When the brigands were gone, Killeen promptly threw herself at the wall of glowing creatures. She reeled back, badly singed. Mikal clutched her leg and begged her not to try again. One word, one gesture from the wizard and the flies would swarm on her, burning her to death.

"You've kept out of my hands a long time, boy," Harlano said, idly circling outside the wall of fire. "You have a certain talent."

"Fate loves me," Mikal answered. He held tight to Killeen.

"No longer."

Footsteps thumped up the far stairs. Everyone turned to see Lyra emerge, brandishing a makeshift club.

"Get back!" she cried. "Leave them alone!"

Harlano smiled. Mikal's heart hardened in fear. With a nod, the wizard dispatched half the swarm of lava flies at Lyra. He knew Harlano meant to kill her. Mikal shouted, but his words were lost when Imolla appeared behind Lyra, arms upraised.

Harlano faltered. The blazing creatures hesitated as well.

"Lava flies, Harlano? Don't you know your fire tricks are no good here?" Imolla said.

She thrust her hands at him. Out of thin air, a deluge of water droplets appeared. The droplets sprouted tiny wings of their own, each one becoming a silver blue butterfly of pure water. Seeing them, Harlano clenched his hands into fists. Lava flies and water flies collided in a burst of steam. When glowing red wings met silver ones, both were annihilated in a puff of vapor.

Imolla swept up another phalanx of water droplets and directed them against the lava flies guarding Mikal and Killeen. No sooner were the two swarms joined,

Killeen vaulted headfirst through them and did a somersault, rolling to her feet in front of Harlano.

"You should have taken the sword," she said.

She seized him by the throat. Harlano melted into smoke. Snarling, Killeen tried to hold on, but the mist dissolved into nothing.

Harlano reappeared many paces away. He called up a fireball in his hands and hurled it at Imolla. She pointed a finger at it. A torrent of water sprayed from her hand. When it struck the blazing fireball, the ball exploded with a shattering bang. The fighting swarms of fiery flies and their wet foes were blown out of existence. Lyra and Mikal were knocked down. Even Killeen was staggered.

"Are you done, rogue?" called Imolla.

Smiling, Harlano produced two fireballs, one in each hand. He hurled them one after the other. His purpose was plain. If Imolla stopped one, the other would get through and strike her.

For a short, round woman Imolla moved quickly. She dodged to one side, lining herself up with the wedge-shaped tomb of Miraco the Mason at her back. The first fireball she blasted with water as before. When it exploded, she threw herself to the floor. The second ball of fire hit the sloping monument and rebounded smartly—right back at Harlano.

He braced himself. As the fireball roared in, he put out his hands to catch it. The ball was just beyond his reach when Imolla raised her hand. She hit the blazing ball when it was right in front of Harlano. It exploded like a clap of thunder.

When Mikal looked up, Harlano was gone. There was a steaming crater in the ancient marble floor.

Lyra ran up. "You got him, Excellent!"

Looking completely exhausted, Imolla braced herself against the girl.

"No," she said. "He's gone, but not far. You must flee. Quickly. He is more powerful than I thought. I cannot hold him much longer."

Killeen helped Mikal stand. They joined Lyra.

"Go where?"

"Atop the dome waits my chariot. It will take you to Tormentall, on the north coast. Master Petruvo will take out that part of Orichalkon's memory that Harlano seeks."

"What will you do, Excellent?" Mikal asked.

"Keep Harlano and his men dancing a while longer." Smiling forlornly, she looped damp strands of hair behind her ears. "I haven't worked this hard in years!"

"I will stand by you," Killeen offered.

"No. Guard the children and the head."

Mikal asked where Orry was. Imolla had already loaded him in her chariot.

Mikal kissed the wizard's hand. She was ice cold, and soaking wet—with sweat or water magic, he could not tell.

Lyra dragged him away. The dome was thick enough to have spiral steps cut inside. Lyra, Mikal, and Killeen pounded up, circling halfway around the enormous dome before they reached the top.

Mighty Killeen heaved against the stone slab that sealed the passage. It shifted, and they found themselves atop the great dome, high above the city of Farhaven.

The wolf-woman paled. Lyra looked ill. She gripped the stone steps hard, showing no signs of wanting to quit the stairwell.

A few steps away sat an elaborate-looking horseless wagon. The high sides were covered in dark red leather. Glass lanterns gleamed on each corner.

"Hurry!" Mikal said. His fear of heights was suddenly gone.

Neither Killeen nor Lyra budged until a loud boom echoed from below. On hands and knees, the girl and wolf-woman crept after Mikal to the waiting chariot.

CHAPTER 13

ONE CASTLE

Wind whipped around them. Mikal scampered over the tile roof, even though a misstep would mean a fast slide off the dome to the city far below. He reached the chariot. There was a door in the side, held shut by a brass hook. He tumbled inside, calling to his friends to join him quickly.

Imolla called this a chariot. Mikal had a dim memory from his reading that a chariot was a small, two-wheeled vehicle drawn by horses. This thing was more like a wheelless wagon.

Orry was at the other end, clamped to a polished brass bracket.

"Fate, I am glad to see you!" Mikal cast about for reins or rudder or some method of guidance. "How does this thing work?"

"It w-works like this."

The leather-bound box rose off the dome. Lyra and Killeen protested.

"Don't leave us behind!" Lyra cried.

"Get in, get in!" Mikal said.

Killeen had just slipped in when lava flies blasted through the trap door. Mikal shouted "Up! Up!" and the chariot staggered off the dome. He latched the door. Lyra and Killeen lay flat on the floor, heads covered with their hands.

"Away, away!" Orry sang out. The chariot hurtled through the air like an arrow. Mikal lost his footing and sprawled on his friends. Lyra recited choice words at his clumsiness.

He groped his way to Orry. "Are you making this fly?"

"No, young m-master, but I d-do seem to b-be guiding it!"

The chariot stood on end, nose pointed at the sky. Mikal, Lyra, and Killeen tumbled to the rear wall in a tangled heap.

"Fly level!" Mikal managed to shout through a tangle of arms and legs. "Level!"

From nose up the chariot pitched nose down, plunging straight for the jagged rooftops of Farhaven. Lyra shrieked as they fell. Killeen held tight to the girl and clenched her eyes shut.

"Orry," Mikal said in the metal head's ear, "Fly level or we're all going to die!"

"I'm t-trying!"

"Try harder!"

Shaking from one end to the other, the flying chariot lifted its nose. They swooped across the rooftops of

Farhaven, smashing chimneys and scraping shingles. Metal eyes jammed wide open, Orry drove the chariot upward at a more gentle angle. Moments later, they were skimming over the harbor. Sailors gaped, and a lookout high on a ship's mast fell backward in amazement as they flashed past.

Mikal slowly stood up. The wind buffeted him, but he braced his feet apart and stood upright.

"Hello!" he called to his cowering companions. "Rise and see where we are going!"

"I know where we're going," Lyra said. Her hands were over her eyes. "We're going to die!"

He left her to her fears. Imolla's strange flying box hurtled over the waves. Mikal had never seen the sea. All sorts of ships, large, small, and in-between, crowded the roadstead. He saw slim galleys, tubby roundships, and tall-masted argosies. It astonished Mikal that there could be so much water in one place. Compared to the sea, the Tombow River was a ditch.

"I would l-like to go h-higher," Orry said, wind stealing the words from his bronze lips.

Mikal saw why. A flock of birds was crossing in front of them. If they kept going as they were, they would crash into them.

"Go as you will," Mikal said. The chariot heaved up, provoking more groans from Lyra.

Orry climbed to what seemed like a great height, well above birds and ships' masts. It was morning, and the sun was at their backs as they flew out to sea. Gradually, Orry brought the craft about northward. The coastline fell behind them until there was nothing below but sea.

Mikal found bags of provisions that Imolla had thoughtfully packed. He gnawed hard biscuit and wondered if she could defeat Harlano. It felt wrong leaving her, battling his old master and Quintane's gang by herself.

Lyra's grimy fingers reached in. He held the bag open for her.

"Thinking about Excellent?" she said. He nodded. "She'll fare well, I'll bet. Wizards are hard to kill." He didn't remind her of the petrified young sorcerer they had found in Woodhaven.

Eventually, Killeen overcame her dread of heights and joined them. Squint-eyed and sweating, she crouched against the side of the chariot taking quick sips from a water bottle. When asked how she was doing, she muttered that she would speak when her feet were on the ground again.

The day passed in a parade of towering clouds. Peeking through the airy islands, the sun followed its ageless course. As it began to settle in the west, Killeen grew restless. Her change was coming. The children had never seen her transform, and they knew she was modest about it. Lyra and Mikal agreed to avert their eyes when the time came.

The sun sank. Mountains appeared on the eastern horizon. Orry banked toward them.

"Th-this is the n-north coast of Peri-Peri-Periskold! Tormentall should b-be b-below!"

There was nothing below but cliffs and crashing surf. Orry descended and slowed. All at once, the castle of Tormentall appeared. Built of the same stone as the steep, jagged cliffs, it was almost indistinguishable from the natural crags.

"That's it?" said Lyra. She managed to peer over the side, but her knuckles were white where she gripped the leather-covered wall. "Looks like a ruin."

It did look dilapidated. Four walls of unequal length enclosed a diamond-shaped courtyard. Tall towers marked the union of each stone wall. Three of the four towers had lost their peaked roofs, and one had tumbled down the cliff to the shore.

Inside the walls was a tall stone keep. No light or life showed.

"Can you come down in the courtyard? Between the wall and the keep?" Mikal said.

"T-too tight," Orry replied. "I'll t-try outside."

A narrow road wound up the hill to the castle. Orry meant to set down in front of the main gate, but tricky winds upset the chariot while he was still airborne. Imolla's chariot touched the ground and tipped sideways. With a creak, the flying box careened over. Mikal, Lyra, and Killeen, in wolf form, tumbled out.

Silently, rain began to fall. After making sure everyone was unhurt, Mikal unbolted Orry from the chariot. Lyra walked up the rubble-stone path to the castle gate. Sleek and gray, Killeen stood at her side.

"What do you think?" said the girl. Killeen loped through the open gate.

Lyra waited for Mikal. Rain was coming down lightly, just dampening their shoulders. Beads of water ran down Orry's dented cranium. They advanced together, puzzled by the dark and lifeless condition of the castle.

The gate stood open. Enormous timbers, as thick as Mikal's waist, were crumbling with rot. The ground was covered with loose stones and bits of rusty metal. Mikal picked up a strip of corroded iron, part of a wagon wheel. He easily snapped it in two.

"Does anyone live in this ruin?" Lyra asked.

Rats did. As they passed through the outer wall, they heard rustling and squealing in the shadows.

The inner courtyard was overgrown with weeds. Sheds and outbuildings around the yard were falling into disrepair. What had happened here? Where was the wizard Petruvo, master of Tormentall castle?

Killeen appeared in the doorway of the keep. She barked, doglike, then darted back inside.

"Do you know anything about this place?" Mikal whispered.

"Castle T-Tormentall was b-built by the counts of T-Tormentall exactly th-three hundred and eleven years ago," Orry recited brightly. "Classified as a m-modified motte and bailey t-type fortification, it was the s-seat of the lords of T-Tormentall until n-ninety-six years ago, when it was d-deeded to the Guild of Constant W-Working. The first G-Guild occupant was the w-wizard Flayda, who—"

"Enough."

They entered the dark doorway. Lyra leaned against the massive portal, shoving it back on rusty hinges. It groaned like a living thing.

"What do you know about Master Petruvo?" Mikal asked Orry.

"Born, D-Darland, Sievegold P-Province, sixty-six y-years ago. Studied under the high m-master Wickoff—"

"Enough."

Petruvo was old. Perhaps that accounted for the poor state of the castle.

They crossed a large hall littered with broken furniture and stands of armor. Lyra found a fine old table with an axe embedded in it. Chair legs, chopped for firewood, were stacked beside the axe. Mikal examined the blade. It was bright. Someone had used it recently.

Like a phantom, Killeen appeared at the top of the stone steps. Behind her was a rosy halo of light. The children smelled wood smoke.

"Is it all right?" Mikal called out. Killeen barked once, and then turned away. He took that to mean yes.

The second floor was totally different from the first—different from the rest of the castle. A large, cheerful fire blazed on the baronial hearth. Massive furniture populated the great room like small fortresses. Mikal and Lyra wandered their way through the tables, beds, and huge chairs to the fire. On the hearth sat an old man with a white beard. He wore a faded red velvet robe, nearly worn through at the knees and elbows. Killeen sat beside him. He was scratching her behind her ears. She evidently enjoyed it.

"Hello," said the old man pleasantly. "Is this your wolf? Marvelous creature."

Lyra folded her arms. "She's a werewolf."

Snow-colored brows rose. "Really? She's so friendly. I thought lycanthropes were consumed with bloodlust."

"Not Killeen," Mikal said. "Not since she met Orry."

"Are you Orry?"

Mikal introduced himself, Lyra, and Orry. The old man's mouth fell open. He held out his hands. Mikal carefully set his metallic friend in the man's bony fingers.

"Orichalkon! To think I lived long enough to hold you in my hands!"

"Who are y-you?" Orry asked.

"You're damaged," said the old man. He turned the head to see the dent. "Recently, too. I can fix that."

"Are you Master Petruvo?" Lyra said.

"Petruvo? No, alas, he died almost a fortier ago. I am Alabaster, his archivist."

CHAPTER 14

FOUR STUDENTS

M ikal's face must have shown his shock. Alabaster stood up, cradling Orry under one arm.

"I am sorry, my boy. Are you a relation of Petruvo's?"

"He was our last hope," Lyra said, sagging into a threadbare chair. "Now we are doomed!"

Alabaster looked helplessly from Lyra to Mikal to Orry. Taking a seat by the fire, Mikal told him the whole story—of Orry, Harlano, their escape across Periskold to Farhaven, and Imolla's plan for Petruvo to remove the information from Orry's memory, making him worthless to Harlano and the Anvil.

"I may be able to help you," Alabaster said at last. "I am no wizard, but I have served at Petruvo's side for long years and know many things."

"Can you take out the knowledge Orry has that Harlano wants?" asked Mikal.

"No, but I should be able to fix your friend."

"What good will that do?" Lyra said.

Alabaster smiled. "If Orichalkon can speak clearly, he may be able to tell us how to expunge the dangerous datum."

Beyond the fireplace, the rear half of the hall was a wondrous workshop. Alabaster lit candles, and every time a flame caught, marvels rose from the shadows. They saw strange, intricate devices made entirely of glass rods, clear as water and hard as ice. Candlelight sparkled on them. Mikal had no clue what they did, but they were beautiful.

They passed tables crowded with strange devices wrought in metal or carved from stone. They weren't figures of people or animals, but simple shapes: cylinders, spheres, pyramids, and cubes, all melded seamlessly together. In reverent whispers, Mikal asked what the objects did.

"Nothing, now," Alabaster said. "It was Petruvo's life work to create sets of identical artifacts, and then distribute them to important members of the Guild."

"Why?" said Lyra.

"To communicate with each other. His dream was that by touching one artifact, the twin would summon its owner so that the two wizards could converse."

Some of the weird sculptures had twins. But others did not.

"Why didn't he send these out?"

Alabaster sighed. "He never sent *any* of them out. Knowing his brother and sister sorcerers, he knew the ones who didn't get their artifacts right away would be jealous of those who did." Jealous wizards were dangerous creatures, Mikal knew. "He kept working until he had a pair of artifacts for every senior magician in the Guild. He died before he could finish the last ones."

Mikal paused by a spiral creation of copper, amber, and obsidian. He touched it lightly. On the next table the identical figurine glowed with life. He snatched his hand away.

"It works!"

"Of course. Master Petruvo was most skilled."

The scope of the wizard's work left Mikal feeling sad. All this work, all this craftsmanship, and what became of it? Nothing.

Near the rear wall of the keep they came to a long table covered with tools. Killeen lay down on the floor, her head on her paws. Alabaster clamped Orry's base to the table and lit the wick of an oil lamp. A silver bell-shaped mirror behind the lamp focused the light on the head.

"Feels g-good," Orry said. "Almost like s-sunlight."

Alabaster examined Orry carefully with a disk of polished glass mounted on a wooden handle. When he passed in front of Lyra and Mikal, they saw everything seen through the disk was made larger. Clever magic.

"The fore part of our friend's cranium is one piece," Alabaster murmured.

Lyra sniffed. "What's that mean?"

"It means, unwashed child, I cannot remove that part of his skull and pound out the dent."

Instead the old man picked up a small hand auger. It was just like the ones Haruld the Joiner used back in Mikal's village, only the bit was much smaller.

"I will bore here. . . . "

In a moment, Killeen had her ivory teeth on Alabaster's wrist. She did not bite, but her movement was so swift and sudden Alabaster was stricken with fright.

"It's all right," Mikal said soothingly. "He won't hurt Orry."

Killeen withdrew without a sound. She resumed her place on the floor, watching the old man carefully with keen dark eyes.

"I will bore a small hole in the damaged area," Alabaster said, voice shaking. The bit was very sharp. It easily made a pinhole in the hard bronze.

"All well?" Mikal asked.

"T-Tickles," said Orry.

Alabaster took two lengths of stiff wire and bent them to match the contours of the dent. He inserted these in the hole he'd bored, then ran them through the center of a small metal tripod braced against Orry's skull. The wires were twisted together around a slender iron rod. Slowly, Alabaster began to turn the rod. The wires went taut. Grunting, he kept twisting. Little by little, the wires underneath the dent pulled the metal up.

"By Fate, that's a neat trick," said Lyra.

When the dent was gone, Alabaster freed the wires. Only the pilot hole remained. He heated silver solder in a small crucible and filled the hole expertly. After a quick polish, the dent was invisible. Orry's only souvenir was a tiny silver dot on his bronze pate.

"So, Orichalkon—how do you feel?"

"Completely magnificent." They all looked at him, waiting for the stutter. Orry obliged them by saying, "'Round and 'round the ragged rascal ran! Shura the shaman sold sixteen sweets."

"Sounds good to me," Lyra said. "Can we eat now?" Killeen stood up.

Mikal said, "Wait." He turned Orry to face him. "The knowledge Harlano wants; where is it?"

"I do not know, young master."

"What's that mean?" Lyra burst out.

"I am aware of what Master Harlano wants. I know I have the information inside me, but I don't know how to speak it. I cannot say it now, to you who are my friends. It is—locked inside, very deeply."

"How would Harlano get the knowledge from you?" said Mikal.

"I know not."

Mikal knew Orry could not lie. He could sometimes not say everything asked of him, but he could not lie outright.

To Alabaster he said, "Master, you have been very kind to us. I hate to ask more work from you, but can you do anything to help us? It's important."

The old man rubbed his lips. After a while he said, "Petruvo left a furnace. It can easily melt bronze."

Orry said nothing. Mikal looked away. What seemed impossible not long ago now seemed like a painful possibility.

"It is all right," Orry said. "Better to melt down than deliver the world into the Anvil's hands."

Lyra said, "Fury knows I hate Harlano, but I'll not see you melted, old head!"

Alabaster rested a hand on Mikal's shoulder. "You must decide," he said. "You and Orichalkon."

The night passed badly for Mikal. Lyra slept noisily on a vast bed. Killeen lay quietly by the fire. Orry and Alabaster sat up late, conversing quietly among Petruvo's wasted artifacts. Mikal heard their murmurs and occasional laughter. Sometime, not long before dawn, he managed to sleep.

Killeen awakened him late. Everyone else was bustling around. Alabaster cooked sausages in the fireplace. Aching and tired, Mikal joined his friends.

"Here he is," Lyra proclaimed, biting a substantial sausage in two. "The sleeping prince."

"Better a prince than a frog," Killeen said.

"Eh?"

"You rumble and rasp through the night like a raft of bullfrogs," the wolf-woman said. "I can barely sleep."

"Oh? Maybe it's all the fleas that keep you awake!"

Alabaster stood between them, holding out a sizzling pan. "Are you hungry?"

Mikal was. They ate well, and Alabaster offered to give them a tour of the castle. The outer works did not take long. Crumbling walls and shaky towers were best admired from solid ground.

"That collapse looks recent," Killeen remarked, pointing at the fallen tower.

"Yes, it was there Petruvo lost his life," Alabaster said. A storm, Mikal wondered?

"The day was clear and bright," the old man told them. "Master Petruvo had a habit of walking the battlements daily, in spite of the perilous state of the masonry. He entered the west tower, as was his wont, and never came out. A mighty wind roared in from the sea, taking the tower down."

The courtyard was partly blocked by the debris. Killeen climbed the cairn. If Petruvo was buried under all this rubble, he was as secure in his grave as any king of Phalia in a marble tomb.

"You say the old wizard walked the walls every day?" Killeen asked. Alabaster, leaning on Mikal's arm, nodded. "I wonder if his death was the pick of Fate, or something else?"

She did not have to explain. Harlano and the Anvil had been busy thinning the ranks of the Guild. Perhaps the wind that took down the west tower was not nature's wind at all.

Somberly, they followed Alabaster inside. Above the second floor where the old man lived they were shown Petruvo's library. Mikal was struck silent with awe. He thought Harlano had a large collection of books and scrolls in Oranbold. Harlano's library was a trifle compared to the mountains of documents in Tormentall Castle. Mikal could not even estimate how many books there were. Ten thousand? A hundred thousand? Beyond five zeroes, Mikal's arithmetic was shaky. It looked like chaos, but Alabaster avowed he knew every heap, every stack and pile. Lyra tested him.

"Find me 'Lives of the Kings of Phalia,' by Klato," she said. Alabaster smiled, disappeared among the dusty mountains of books, and returned shortly with a neatly wound scroll. Mikal spread the page and saw the title: The *True and Verified* LIVES *of the most noble* MONARCHS *of the land of* Phalia, *with notes on the throne of* Darland. *By* KLATO, *scribe to* His MAJESTY Edfold the Fourth.

Impressed, Mikal asked for obscure magical texts, like the forbidden book of Rustava Prondo, Sage of Filorus. Alabaster was delayed no longer finding this rare book. Nothing Lyra or Mikal asked for bothered the archivist more than a little. Laughing, they tried to make up silly titles to confound Alabaster. Killeen spoke up.

"Are there books here about Orry? Books that tell of his making?"

Mikal's grin vanished. Of course! Killeen had seen right to the heart of the problem. Mikal asked Alabaster if he knew of any books on Orry.

"Not that I know of. I do have the works of Sungam the Smith, but they are not complete—"

Lyra and Mikal leaped off the stacks of books they'd been sitting on and took Alabaster by the arms.

"Show us," Lyra said. "Come, white beard, show us!"

"I don't know if it will do any good—"

"Nothing will do no good at all!" Mikal replied.

Into the towering piles of parchment they went. Petruvo's hoard contained no less than one hundred sixty-six books on or by the great wizard, Sungam the Smith. Some were bound tomes, others scrolls copied from far more ancient texts. Then there were many loose sheets of foolscap, shed from books so old the bindings had rotted to dust. Dismayed by the sheer size of the archive, Mikal sat down and took the top page of the nearest pile. Lyra did the same. Alabaster joined in, too.

"Can you read?" he asked Killeen.

"Alas, no."

"I can!" said Orry. "You turn the pages, dear Killeen, and I shall read them!"

They settled down in silence, broken only by Orry's occasional command: "Next!"

CHAPTER 15

FIVE HUNDRED LEAGUES

now came the third day. No one much noticed. From breakfast to bedtime, they read their way through a mountain of ancient texts. Mikal kept a rough tally: They waded through three languages, six dialects, and nine different styles of penmanship. They even found documents in cipher, which not even Alabaster could read. Mikal hoped to Fate the answer they sought was not concealed in them.

On a trip to the well in the courtyard one morning, Killeen brought back word the snow was now calf-deep. She went out to Imolla's abandoned chariot, meaning to drag it inside the castle. She saw something that caused her to retreat quickly to the keep.

"What did you see?" Lyra said.

"Footprints in the snow."

Mikal set aside the scroll he was studying. "How many people, do you think?"

"Just one. Wearing boots."

Alabaster wasn't worried. "Some passing shepherd saw Excellent Imolla's conveyance and took a closer look. I'm sure that's all it was."

The children accepted the old man's theory. Even so, Killeen did not return to the chariot.

On the fourth morning of their stay at Tormentall, Mikal heard Alabaster grumbling around the hearth. When he asked, Alabaster said his grocer was late.

"Woz hasn't been late in lo, seven years. Every tenth day he comes out in his cart, bringing provisions. I wonder where he could be?"

"Snow," said Lyra, joining the conversation. She gnawed a chicken leg left over from last night's supper. "It's getting deep out there."

Alabaster frowned. "That must be it."

Two days more, and their food was dwindling fast. Killeen offered to go out at night and run down a few hares. Everyone agreed, though Mikal said, "Keep out of the farmers' yards."

The wolf-woman's eyes glinted in the firelight. "I never go in yards. Sometimes livestock strays."

Killeen departed in wolf form after sunset. Mikal sat propped against a stately old chair, carved with the crest of the Counts Tormentall. He was plowing through a dreary treatise by Sungam, with commentaries by the later wizard Flayda. The Smith's words were penned in reddish-brown ink on the left page of a bound book. Flayda's comments were in black on the facing page. In the midst of a long explanation of the virtue of fire in purifying magical objects, Flayda had written:

Here the sage omits what he should reveal, namely, how to bind knowledge and word in brightworked metal. He did so with great success with Brazen Top [Orry!], binding the wisdom of many ages of natural philosophy into the cogs of Its memory. . . .

Mikal leaped to his feet. "Look here!"

Alabaster and Lyra looked up. From the girl's red-rimmed eyes, he knew she had been dozing.

He showed them the passage. "Orry's knowledge is stored in the cog wheels in his head!"

"That's sounds right," said Alabaster. "But which one holds the secret of the Brightstone?"

Orry had hundreds of wheels, large and small, fitted with extreme precision inside his bronze skull. What they needed now was a list of the wheels and what each one contained—if such a list existed.

Mikal set Orry on a table between a pair of candelabras.

"Do you know your knowledge is stored on gear wheels inside your head?" he said.

"I do if you tell me so."

"Can you sort them, in place? Ask yourself, what is on this cogwheel?"

Click-clack. Orry blinked slowly. "I will have to start at the beginning."

Lyra peered over Mikal's shoulder. "How many wheels have you got?"

Orry's eyes closed. "Two thousand, seven hundred and eighty-eight."

Lyra snorted with disgust. Mikal patted Orry and told him to begin.

"Wheel one, class one, region one . . . " There was a louder than usual whirr inside Orry's head. "Words . . . diction . . . rules of spelling . . . of the Wenzeland tongue." Sungam came from Wenzeland.

"*Yo osti manka*," Orry recited.

"What does that mean?"

"'I am a girl.'"

"Oh Fury," Lyra said. "This will take forever!"

"Go on," Mikal said. He took Lyra by the arm and led her away. Back among Petruvo's books they found Alabaster asleep, one blunt finger resting on the page he had been reading. Mikal draped a blanket around the old man's shoulders.

"You sleep, too," he told Lyra. "There's no reason we must all blind ourselves reading. Orry will sort it out."

Lyra yawned. "In a fortier or two. Good night."

Alone, Mikal tried to keep reading, but the cold silence of the old keep closed in on him. The fire died down, and he began to see vapor pluming from his nose. He got up to put a log on the fire.

Mikal stopped like a statue. Lying on the floor just inside the glow of the hearth was Killeen, as a wolf. The pale gray fur of her hindquarters were stained red. The stump of an arrow shaft stuck out of her right leg.

He fell on his knees. Killeen opened one eye and gently licked Mikal's hand with her black tongue.

"What happened?" he gasped.

Had she run into an angry farmer? Farmers didn't carry bows. A hunter, stalking deer in the snowy uplands of the coast?

He touched the broken arrow lightly. Killeen growled deep in her throat. Mikal snatched his hands back.

"Sorry!" He went to wake Alabaster.

Killeen's condition shocked the old man, too. How had she managed to get shot with a crossbow bolt in the middle of the night?

"How do you know it's a crossbow bolt?" Mikal asked. The shaft was too thick for any hand-held bow, Alabaster said, examining it.

He rummaged through some cupboards and found a potion for pain. Killeen let Alabaster put the mouth of the vial between her teeth. She swallowed. A moment later, she sighed.

"I'll sit on her head," Alabaster said in a low voice. "You pull the shaft out."

Mikal wanted to protest, but he merely nodded. The old man took Killeen's head in his lap. He clamped both hands around her powerful jaws. Now was the time. Mikal grasped the broken bolt. He counted to himself, one, two, three! Pulling as hard as he could, he yanked the missile out in one swift movement.

Killeen thrashed through the medicine, breaking Alabaster's grip with ease. Mikal scrambled backward.

She staggered upright, but the drug and her wound would not let her stand. Down she went.

"That potion would numb a snow bear," Alabaster said, awed.

They washed Killeen's wound and bound it well with strips of linen. Alabaster examined the bolt by candlelight. It had an iron broadhead and no markings. It could have come from anywhere.

They carried Killeen to the hearth. Alabaster covered her with a fluffy sheepskin rug.

"We'll wait till morning and ask her what happened," he said.

Judging by how much the candles had burned down, morning wasn't far off. Tired as he could be, Mikal took a bucket out to the well. The sky was gray with dawn. Snow in the courtyard was knee-deep. As Mikal prepared to drop the bucket down the well, he heard voices shouting in the distance from the sea-side of the castle.

He left the bucket and started up the steep steps to the battlement. The stone was treacherous in fine weather. Coated with snow, they were deadly. Mikal slipped many times. Once, near the top, he almost fell backward off the wall. Fate was still on his side, and he gained the battlement at last.

The sea was the color of slate, topped with whitecaps. Above, a lowering sky nearly the same color had merged into the dark water. Rising and falling with the waves were four long ships with furled sails and a row of bristling oars.

Small boats dotted the sea between the ships. They were rowing hard for shore. The boats were crowded with men. From his high perch, Mikal could see they wore steel helmets. Bare swords and spear points glittered among the packed ranks.

Whoever they were, they did not look friendly—and they were coming ashore. Mikal skittered down the steps. He ran hard through the snow, into the keep and shut the door. An ironclad bar stood in a niche behind the door. Mikal struggled to get it in place, barring the door.

"Alabaster! Lyra! Killeen! Men outside! Soldiers—warriors! Coming this way!"

Groggy, Lyra and Alabaster met him by the archive door. He told them about the ships and men. Alabaster's amber eyes widened. He dashed downstairs to the great hall. Lyra and Mikal followed. From an old cupboard, the old man fetched a small brass box. Inside was what looked like a brick of sun-dried clay. Alabaster poked at the hall fireplace until he got a few flames going. He dropped the little brick in the flames. Soon, thick red smoke boiled out of the brick, coiling its way up the flue.

"One of Master Petruvo's last makings," Alabaster said. "To protect the castle."

As the brick slowly turned to smoke, Mikal heard booms and clangings throughout the castle. Petruvo's magic block was sealing Tormentall against intruders. The gates shut themselves, hardening their rotten timber as they did. Stones grew together like vines, windows shrank to slits, and holed roofs became sound again.

No sooner had Alabaster sealed Tormentall castle, when resounding blows thundered through the keep. Apparently the intruders, whoever they were, had reached the now-closed gate.

"To the Oratory," Alabaster said. This was the highest room in the keep. "We can see what's going on from there."

Along the way, they found Killeen (now a woman) sitting upright by the fire in the library. She had the sheepskin rug close around her. Because she had transformed in her sleep inside the castle, she had not been able to dress after her change.

"Killeen, there are men outside," Mikal said, panting.

"I know. One of them shot me last night."

"Did you see who it was?"

"It was the man we saw with the wizard in Imolla's round room."

Quintane!

She ran a hand over the rug covering her leg. "He could have killed me, but didn't. He wounded me on purpose." Her wolf senses had failed to detect Quintane. He must have been masked by magic. That meant Harlano was near.

"If Quintane and old baldy were outside last night, why didn't they come in after us? And who are the men from the sea?" Lyra wondered.

Mikal had no idea. Maybe the soldiers coming ashore would help them. But who would send armed men and ships to aid Mikal and his friends?

A loud boom echoed through the keep. It was repeated, again and again. Someone was battering the restored gate.

"The chariot—where is it?" Lyra was ready to fly away again.

"Outside," Killeen said through clenched teeth. "On its side, full of snow."

Alabaster started for the workshop end of the hall. When Mikal called after him, asking him where he was going, the old man replied, "To light the furnace."

A lump grew in Mikal's throat. Lyra said a single oath, then went the opposite way from Alabaster. There were swords and other weapons in the ground floor hall, heaps of them. She was going to arm herself.

She was brave in her way, and stubborn to a fault, but Mikal knew they could not hold out against a band of ruthless brigands. He clattered down the steps behind her.

The hall below was cold and dark. Petruvo's potion had sealed the building, so only the slimmest beams of sunlight pierced the interior. Lyra rooted through the rusty, forgotten arms littering the floor. Mikal was about to speak when a mighty blow hit the front door of the keep.

The intruders were inside the castle. They had already breached the main gate.

Lyra waddled past, carrying an assortment of weapons. "Go on, load up!" she grunted.

He felt foolish hefting a warlord's sword and shield. Spotting a spear, he dropped the sword and retreated upstairs. Mikal was only halfway up when the keep door burst apart. Chunks of timber and broken iron straps showered the hall. A blast of icy air followed.

Through the shattered door came Harlano, flanked by Quintane. A small group of brigands trailed them. They were quickly shouldered aside by the well-armed men Mikal had seen landing from the ships.

Bowstrings creaked. A dozen arrows were drawn and aimed at Mikal. He dropped the heavy spear and held the shield up with both shaking hands.

"Hold," Harlano said. "Where is the head?"

"Melted down!" Mikal shouted. "He's a puddle of molten bronze by now!"

"Boy, if that is true, your life and the lives of anyone in this castle are done." Harlano pointed up the stairs. "Well, go on, find the head!"

The ships' landing party rushed the steps. They flowed around Mikal, all but trampling him. After the first men reached the next floor, he heard Lyra's shrill voice. A clatter of steel and rough laughter followed. One of the warriors returned, holding Lyra at arm's length by the back of her blouse. She was cursing hard enough to make smoke come out her ears. The grinning soldier dumped her beside Mikal. He saw the man had a gash on his cheek. Lyra had scored, if only a scratch.

Harlano, Quintane, and what remained of the brigands slowly mounted the steps. Pausing by the boy and girl, Quintane said, "May I cut their throats now, my lord?"

"Not until I have the head."

The ruffians grabbed Mikal and Lyra by the hair and forced them upstairs. When they reached the next floor, they found the entire company of warriors held up by Killeen. Lyra had given her a crossbow. Somehow she managed to load and cock it. Sitting on the hearth, wrapped in sheepskin, she had the entire invasion at bay.

"What are you waiting for?" Harlano said. "You're paid to take this place. Will you let yourself be stopped by a wounded woman with a single crossbow?"

"They have good sense," Killeen replied. "Only one will die, but no one wants to volunteer for the job."

"Rush her," Quintane said. "She won't hit anyone."

At that, Killeen leveled the bow and put her only bolt into Quintane's heart. He blinked, astonished, and fell dead.

In a flash the soldiers seized Killeen, disarming her. She might have fought them, but seeing Mikal and Lyra in their hands, she gave up. Quintane's men wanted to avenge their leader. Harlano said no.

He studied her closely. Killeen was taller than Harlano, even in her bare feet.

"You're the lycanthrope," he said. "Interesting." To the warriors he said, "Bind her well with chains on hands and feet. Take her to my ship."

"What are you going to do with her?" Lyra cried.

"Where I am going she will fetch a good price."

Mikal said, "Where are you going?" Harlano did not answer.

The soldiers ranged through the keep in pairs, smashing Petruvo's delicate artifacts and upending furniture. In the workshop they flushed Alabaster. The old man's face was streaked with soot. He was sweating and trembling.

Harlano smiled. "Where is the Sungam head?"

Wordlessly, Alabaster pointed. A thick crucible sat atop a furnace. Fire rumbled inside.

"I melted it, to keep it from your hands!" Alabaster declared.

Harlano's face darkened. For a moment, Mikal thought he would throttle Alabaster with his own hands. But he peeked into the glowing pot. His pale brows bunched together. Smiling, he stepped back from the raging heat.

"A good try," he said, "but not good enough. That is not Sungam's bronze head."

"It is!"

"I owned the head for years before I knew its worth. There's enough metal in it to fill two crucibles that size. That is not the head."

Everyone was watching Harlano so intently they forgot to keep good hold of Mikal and Lyra. Lyra stomped the foot of the thug holding her arm. He howled and hopped away. Mikal elbowed his captor in the gut and sprang loose, too. They ran in opposite directions.

Harlano barked, "Forget them! The head is all that matters!"

A burly warrior twisted Alabaster's arm behind his back. The old man gasped in pain. Mikal crawled under a heavy table and waited to see if he was being chased. No one came after him, so he crawled in the shadows to the far stairs that went up to the Oratory, at the top of the keep.

From his place, Mikal saw the men shove Alabaster to the main stairs. He hurried to the side steps to keep up.

The Oratory had a high-beamed ceiling. It was deathly cold up there. Dust lay thick on what little furniture remained. The dust betrayed Alabaster more than his pain. Harlano was able to follow his tracks in the dust to a large chest. He threw open the lid and smiled. In went the wizard's hand. When he stood up, he held Orry aloft for all to see.

"Orichalkon. It is good to see you."

"Wheel 494 contains weather records for Florian and other southern islands. The prevailing temperature is balmy, which aids in the growth of three crops a year—"

"Still spouting nonsense, are you? You'll see the weather in Florian soon enough. There you will spout everything I want to know. Won't you?"

"—renowned for its dates and red wines. The island of Phrasca is best known for its cotton—"

Poor Orry. Mikal knew when he was nervous he tended to jabber. Harlano put Orry in a black velvet bag and gave him to a warrior with gold leaves on his helmet.

"Guard that with your life."

Wind whistled through the window shutters. Harlano looked at windows at the far end of the Oratory. He drew on fur-lined gloves. Gesturing to his men, he sauntered to the rattling shutters. The soldiers dragged Alabaster with them.

Harlano lifted a rusty latch with one finger and pushed the shutters apart. Raw wind entered, causing even the stoutest warrior to shudder.

"Bleak place," said Harlano. "I never understood why the Guild wanted this drafty old pile. It was cold the day I visited Petruvo. I offered him a place with us, but the old fool refused."

Harlano put a foot on the sill. "It didn't take much to topple that rotten old tower."

Alabaster looked down. Below, in the courtyard, were the remains of the fallen tower. As he looked at the tomb of his old friend and master, Harlano put a hand to his back. Without a warning smile he gave the old man a shove. Alabaster slipped through the window with only a short yelp. Harlano kept looking out the window a while longer. Satisfied, he closed the shutters and latched them.

From his hiding place, Mikal stifled a sob. Hot tears coursed down his face. Harlano and his men filed out.

Mikal stayed where he was a long time. It wasn't until he heard Lyra calling that he stirred.

"Up here!"

She appeared on the main stairs. "I was thinking you were dead," she said.

"Alabaster is. Is Harlano gone?"

She led him to the other end of the Oratory. Through a crack in the shutter they could see the four ships were hoisting aboard their landing parties. The ship closest to shore ran a flag up its mast.

"Phrasca," Lyra whispered. "Those pirates are from the island of Phrasca."

"Is Phrasca near Florian?"

Lyra nodded. "Florian is a big island. Phrasca is a smaller island across the strait."

"We're going to Florian," Mikal declared.

"Florian? Why not to Phrasca?"

He explained what he overheard Harlano say to Orry about the weather in Florian.

Mikal took Lyra by the hand. "However long it takes, we will find Orry and take him back."

She winced. "Killeen, too?"

He nodded. Gazing at the slowly retreating quartet of ships, Mikal swore a silent oath that all wrongs would be righted and all prisoners would be freed.